The Foreigner

The Foreigner

JACINTA SEQUENTEZ

Petals Publishing Ltd
2016

First published in Great Britain in 2016 by
Petals Publishing Ltd

This book is a work of fiction. Names, characters, places and incidents, other than those clearly in the public domain, are fictitious, and any resemblance to actual events or locales or to real persons, living or dead, is purely coincidental.

A CIP catalogue record for this book is available from the British Library

ISBN: 978-0-9955400-0-2 (sc)
ISBN: 978-0-9955400-1-9 (e)

Petals Publishing Ltd
27 Old Gloucester Street London WC1N 3AX
Registered company 10182894
www.petalspublishing.co.uk

Because of the dynamic nature of the Internet, any web addresses or links contained in this book may have changed since publication and may no longer be valid. The views expressed in this work are solely those of the author and do not necessarily reflect the views of the publisher, and the publisher hereby disclaims any responsibility for them.

Any people depicted in stock imagery provided by Thinkstock are models, and such images are being used for illustrative purposes only. Certain stock imagery © Thinkstock.

Lulu Publishing Services rev. date: 8/18/2016

DEDICATION

For the lovely people of Cebu, and of the Philippines:
home will always be home.

ACKNOWLEDGEMENTS

To family members who supported me through tough times and encouraged my writing aspirations, I thank you.

This project has been completed with Lulu's excellent pre-publish expertise. I convey my gratitude and look forward to our next project.

ONE

I am fifteen-years-old when I get it.

'It.' The time a girl becomes a woman. The moment the pain demon hijacks her life for a few days each month. Spears her with excruciating pain. And mess. Well, that's how it is for me.

Why? If God is so real, why does He bestow upon us such a burden? Some days I can't go to school. I can't reach my shoe laces. I can't play sport. Some days I can't even get out of bed. I learn to accept it, as we all do, but only with my school nurse's sympathy and pain relief medication. I also learn to apply mind-over-matter techniques, but they are never powerful enough to override the next month's warnings.

I often wish I could have been frozen in time where the innocence of a twelve-year-old is deemed old enough to be accepted as an adult, but still, in parents' eyes, young enough to be treated as a child. For me, that is the best of both worlds; the memorable age of our inclusion in family conversations beyond the familiar call of: you kids off to bed now, it's way past your bedtime; the age where we're invited to adopt adult chores like cooking and going to the mall on our own; and the age where we begin to comprehend the adult conversations and squabbles that previously flew over our head. But still we enjoy our favourite children's games like hopscotch and knuckles, and the TV shows where we dance around the room believing that we'll be the next hip-hop sensation or pop star discovered by a talent scout who just happens to walk past our window as our voice floats across a tiny community with the sweetness of an operatic soprano dreaming her own dream of performing in Les Miserables.

All right, I hear you. You're saying that at fifteen I am a late developer. So I've been told. So what? That's how I am and I'm sure there's many just like me. I never knew when 'it' would happen. It's just like a migraine, isn't it? One moment you're following your carefree daily routine and the next minute you're felled by the most debilitating pain ever imagined – as if the school bully had thrust his fist right through your stomach until it shattered your spine. I wish my mama would have taken me aside for one of those mother / daughter heart-to-hearts about impending body changes – but my mama has never taken me aside for anything. We are further apart than the North and South poles, and just as cold. We are the proverbial chalk and cheese.

In contrast, my papa and I are close. I don't know whether that's a legacy of being his first-born, or the fact that of four siblings, I am the only girl. I have always been favoured; a little extra pocket-money – concealed from my brothers of course; his overlooking my raiding the cookie jar when my poor brothers get smacked for the same indiscretion; and later outfitting me in the best school uniform while the boys wore discards from budget shops and markets, and for the younger two – hand-me-downs. But we are not close enough for papa to discuss those womanly things. Fathers just don't do that.

Of course I know things are happening within me. My chest has risen from the flat runway of Mactan Airport to the undulations of Chocolate Hills in Borocay. My skinny hips have ripened to appetising curves. My legs have grown. And grown. Within months I have morphed from a sinewy child to a curvy, developed woman.

Changes also take place within me. Unexplainable feelings. And thoughts. Thoughts of fingertips brushing over my body, like rustling autumn leaves etching excitement into every pore of my flesh. At first, I do not know what the excitement is, or even what it means – until one night, I become a leaf. And then I know. Trapped in a corner by a stiff breeze, I rock sublimely to and fro, my surrounds indecipherable as delight and ecstasy surge through me. Seasons pass through me. The crinkled leaves swirl and crackle within my soul, like effervescent bubbles trampolining inside a glass of Coke. I sear to pillar-box red as primal urges rush like torrents after a winter's downpour. I am wet with discovery. An electrical storm pulsates energy through my toes – they waver to and fro like a stand of pines waltzing in a brief squall.

Summer's heat radiates from my body. No longer am I a rustling leaf. I am a woman.

My interests change too. Gone is my love of dolls, hop-scotch and candy. Correction. My love of candy remains. But I inherit new loves. Boys, boys and boys. And that's when my mama becomes weird. Or weirder. She starts warning me about boys. I ponder her strange behaviour: never before has she broached the subject, not even when I used to play stones – the poor family's version of mar-bles – with little Ricardo from next door. Mama said: 'Don't be spending too much time with boys. They not good for you. They get you into trouble.'

'Into trouble?' I questioned. 'What do you mean?'

'Never mind. One day I tell.'

I'd never been in trouble before and could not imagine how a boy would get me 'into trouble.'

It was not until the following weekend, when talking to my best friend Mae, that I understood what mama had really meant. Surely she didn't think I was going to let a boy do *that*. I must have been so naïve to have not realised the subject mama was hedging around – I feel sort of stu-pid about it now. Of course we talk about all that stuff at school; it just did not click with me that my mama, who rarely discusses anything of a personal nature, would proffer a cloaked warning about participating in sexual frivolity.

I must tell you about Mae. She is one of those girls we meet through the family network and remain friends for evermore. In our case, Mae and I met as six-year-olds at our local pre-school. From there, we have shared school and family like de facto sisters. There is nothing we haven't shared with each other and nothing we won't do to stave off moments of crisis.

———————

One Saturday, I accompany Mae to a nearby internet café, one of thousands scattered throughout the Philippines. I confess that I'd never used one because all my family and friends interact through texts and the occasional phone call when we have a few surplus pesos.

I glance around the congested, stuffy little shop full of whirring computer terminals whose screens flicker and flash like a polytechnic light show. Coiled wires dangle behind tables and stretch their way to overloaded power points parasitically protruding from the wall. Cheap plastic chairs, some sporting chipped and broken legs, straddle two computer bays, challenging the next customers to duel for their possession. Young boys click keyboards to the commands of online games; their bodies swaying side to side, driving cars, piloting planes, dodging bullets and evading prehistoric monsters. Young girls click keyboards, view pages of online profiles, flutter into webcams, type life stories into chat screens and try to evade predatory monsters.

'What are looking at,' I ask.

'The best way to meet a foreigner,' Mae replies. She clicks her recently uploaded 'profile'. I study the page professing her great qualities, some of which I'm sure she's created solely for the purpose of membership. Like

5

many girls, Mae has adjusted her date of birth to eighteen-years-old to meet the website's eligibility criteria. Three photos gleam from the monitor, one very risqué. Good word, that, isn't it? I learnt it in English only a week ago – turns out to be French. Anyway, I think she must have snapped the photo in her bedroom behind closed doors. I'm positive her mama would not approve of her daughter exposing half a breast 'accidentally' unrestrained by her lace-trimmed red bra. A model would pass off such a faux pas as a 'wardrobe malfunction.' To me, I think it cheapens my friend and makes her look desperate. Concerned for her reputation I voice my opinion: 'That's a bit, sort of, you know, too much to show isn't it?'

'Nah. Not on here. You get all the good guys that way.'

She clicks to the next page which bullet-points the qualities she seeks in a man. I'm one who roughs out a list before going shopping, but never have I thought of specifying the qualities I want in a boyfriend. Mae's list is an education in itself. I've seen recipes with fewer ingredients. Grammarians dub it 'poetic licence.' For example, what seventeen-year-old Filipina would find compatibility with man interested in Chaucer, Sappho and Renaissance art? I'm sure she's scanned an encyclopaedia to pluck historical characters and events that she believes will feature in intellectual conversations. Me? I'd just list cooking, watching the latest American soaps and following the newest, gorgeous up-and-coming boy band.

Mae tells me how the internet is the best way for a girl to hook up, especially with a foreigner. As the daughter of a mixed marriage, Mae knows her mama married an American in 1988. In pre-internet times, women submitted photos accompanied by brief details to agencies that promoted catalogues of girls seeking pen pals, friendship or matrimony. The catalogues were freely distributed, but exorbitant fees were paid by gentleman (they were always 'gentlemen', never 'guys') who wanted to respond to his chosen girl. Various scales of charges applied per contact or per letter. Either way, the generically named introduction agency (so named to hamper authorities' investigations of the cash-sapping businesses) would flourish regardless of whether or not the match was successful. Women lost hope and faith in the agency. Men lost money and faith in the agency. That is not to say that all agencies were disreputable. Very few, however, retained the same business name for longer than twelve months.

From such bright prospects and opportunities grew the derogatory term 'Mail Order Bride'. The term itself is somewhat of a misnomer, for no person can simply select a photo and order a particular woman. And the woman would hardly be likely to unassumingly walk into such an arrangement – unless she is prepared to do anything to remove herself from an already abusive relationship. For some people, the grass is always greener on the other side.

Strict regulations govern the granting and processing of fiancée and spouse visas. Most countries' immigration departments are fully accountable for migration figures, so great emphasis is placed on ensuring all visa applications are bona fide.

Persons applying to the United States of America for a Class 730 Visa which grants permission for a non-citizen to marry and remain in America, undergo a long application process. Great Britain's process is much shorter with their Fiancée Visa applications being granted, generally, within three to four months. The fiancée will then be permitted to enter and remain in England, on the proviso that she marries her sponsor within six months of arrival. She may, after two years' residence – conditional upon her still being married – apply for citizenship.

I ask Mae how she knows all this and she tells me: 'Research. I've looked into it. You just click on a site to find out about, say, a visa, and you get all the extra information as well – it just depends whether you're bothered to read it or not. I found out the history about the catalogues because my mama told me about them. She even showed me one that included her photo. I sort of felt sorry for her trying to find love in that way, until I realised that it's no different than what I'm doing – the method's just updated.

Mae's parents met after friendship blossomed over 11 months of letters and expensive international phone calls. She now favours mixed marriage, preferring a Caucasian partner over a Philippine national. Perhaps her parents' happiness influenced her to venture outside her own race. Such decisions, then and now, might be founded upon material desires rather than heartfelt emotion. But how often do we see materialism form the catalyst of both love and affection?

Many hearts have shattered in the wake of failed internet romances. Mae relays examples of men asking her to do private things that she would never do anywhere. As a result of bad experiences, she learnt that those men do not seek long-term relationships; they set out only to deceive and exploit young women solely to fulfil their own depraved desires. Some of her friends had taken advantage of such situations and extorted money from eager men, convincing them that they were their 'one and only.' The rorts escalated to acquiring gifts and money from others who believed they were in a serious, monogamous relationship. But they were not, and far from it. Such is the internet – a simmering pot of scams.

TWO

I GUESS THERE'S NO SHAME in admitting that I've long yearned for a boyfriend. After we shy away from dress-ups and animated cartoon shows, we direct our focus to movie stars, boy bands and the good looking guy who hangs around the local mall. We accept that our mind changes course from trying to repel boys to my present manner of wishing the most eligible guys in school would just show a smidgen of interest in me.

As for extrovert genes, I've been short-changed. I am shy and withdrawing – or so goes Mae's assessment. I cannot sidle up to a guy in the cafeteria queue and seductively brush against him in the hope of him turning around and being instantly captivated by my presence. Perhaps such a thought does make me sound desperate. Not a chance. I just feel that emerging womanhood has conquered me. Maybe it's all that hormone stuff, you know, God's will for procreation. Sometimes I think I'm obsessed with finding a boyfriend, sort of as if my life is ruled by one goal. But it's a goal I've rationally set.

There's also the peer-pressure of close friends and class-mates who share lunch breaks with boyfriends, spend half of the weekend in their company and then when home alone, think about the next date and the next kiss.

I want to be much more than a minor acquaintance or a glittering attachment on a guy's arm. I want a real guy with whom I can share interests and dreams; a guy who will close the door on never-ending weekends of emptiness; a guy I can snuggle into when I need warmth, security and compassion; and I want a guy I can share simple things with, like a Chicken Joy in Jollibee's or sitting cross-legged on a blanket sipping a glass of Coke under a palm tree in the park. I guess I also want a guy I won't fight with like I do with my overprotective brothers.

Aah, my brothers. I suppose every young girl would love the protection of a big brother; a brother they can look up to and learn the secrets of the male mind-set. Then again, perhaps that's a secret we'll *never* unlock. One of my brothers, Jacob, follows me home from school – at a distance – just to ensure my safety. Admirable quality, sure, but when one day a fellow student raced up beside me and slung his arm around my waist, Jacob was there in a flash: 'Hi sis. Do you think papa would like to meet this new boy of yours?' I could have kicked him in the ant hole – or worse. My friend of twenty-seven seconds simply said: 'See ya, Jac,' and headed off with his bag swishing across his back like an erratic windscreen wiper.

Anyway, I'm going off track. So excited am I about the prospects of the internet, I ask Mae to construct me a profile similar to hers. Well, not *exactly* similar.

I offer a selection of favourite photos stored in my phone.

'We can't use those,' she says. 'They might satisfy the Passport Office, but they sure won't attract a guy.'

Her attitude disarms me. 'What's wrong with them? Papa said they look great.'

'My point exactly,' Mae replies. 'If something's good enough for your papa, then it's obviously far too ordinary to arouse the interest of a future boyfriend. Just leave it to me.'

'That's what I'm frightened of.' But I do.

We arrange for Mae to take what she calls 'special' photos of me at her home. I sure hope they won't be *too* special because there is no way known that I'll pose half topless for anyone.

Later in the day, Mae refreshes my make-up before we venture outside to access added 'luminance'.

'Luminance? What the heck are you talking about?'

'Lighting Cin'. That's what the pros call it.'

'And since when were you a pro, if you'll pardon the expression?'

'Since the moment you engaged me to fix your love-life.'

Mae throws me a pale yellow chamois top. It looks like a car cleaning rag with two straps. I step back inside and slip the flimsy piece of fabric over my head before threading its laces through awaiting eyelets peeping between my breasts. It's not the look I want.

'Not like that. Leave it undone,' Mae roars.

'No way!' I exclaim, staring at the acre of exposed flesh beckoning all to the wonders of my body.

I don't know that Mae has already planned to protect my modesty: 'Turn to the left just a little.' The shadow of a nearby tree drops a thick black line into the valley of my chest like the swift stroke of an artist's airbrush transforming a triple X photo to one suitable for general publication. 'It's all about illusion and expectation,' she says. 'It's not what you show – it's the dream of what someone wants to see.'

I then wonder why Mae's so contradictory with her display of nearly everything.

She snaps away to the rhythm of her instructions: 'Head to the side'; 'Twist your shoulders and arch your back'; 'Pout your lips.' She sounds pretentious and over the top as she wields the Samsung Galaxy with an eight mega pixel camera capability, which is far from conducive to award winning photography. I am surprised to see the collection of shots produces a semi-professional portfolio that admirably captures my five-feet-four-inch frame. The yellow top complements my white shorts which accentuate my naturally tanned legs – despite my being paler than most Filipinos.

I've often considered the possibility of an American having been grafted onto my family tree. I've also wondered if a searing flash of lightning severed the errant branch and sent it crashing to the ground. Now, all that survives is a scar upon its host. Of course, other branches know one of their number is missing – the tree is lop-sided – but never will they discover the truth of their being until the trunk reveals all.

Perhaps such a scar is scorched into our family tree. Perhaps my grandma had once engaged in a secret dalliance with an American Marine during shore leave? Perhaps my mother, like Mae's, is the by-product of an American fling. I pledge to one day muster sufficient nerve to ask her, or get Mae to help me with Family Tree research.

My photo appears as a sepia silhouette of a 50s movie star. Mae has captured only my head and shoulders – to maximise my beauty, she says – rather than display me as a shrunken image in a backyard family snap. My hair shines on my shoulders, and my half-smile invites the audience's inquisition: *I wonder what's behind that persona?* I could be Lauren Bacall, Katherine Hepburn or Joan Crawford. Mae allows a twist of sun to set upon my face, highlighting thin arched brows sitting like a portico above my dark brown eyes which beam beneath metallic mauve eye shadow, beckoning all to their splendour: 'Yes, Jacinta's the one. Jacinta Sequentez.'

Sorry, how absent-minded of me. I should have introduced myself earlier. Jacinta Sequentez. Bit of a mouthful, isn't it? I nearly changed it at school to a simple name like Mary Roxas or Ann Santos. Then I came to realise that my name is sort of unique, even movie-starish maybe.

What I hate though, is when people shorten it to 'Jac' as in the male name. Some people do not consider the consequences when messing around with friends' names. They take it upon themselves, with no consultation – or permission, mind you – to abbreviate even the shortest name. Heck, I'm guilty of it too. Mae's name is probably one of the shortest I know of, yet I'll occasionally call her 'M'. And true, I've never asked *her* permission.

I don't want to sound over literate, but the name 'Mae' is only one syllable, as is 'M', so I have no idea why I shortened the former. Maybe it's one of those things we do to anoint our closest company with a bit of individualism; to set them aside from others. I know a San, a Bec, a Trace and even a guy called Nat. His tag's the weirdest of all because if in a crowd you heard the name 'Nat' called out, you'd expect to see a sweet girl called Natalie answer the shout. But wait. This guy's not even Nathaniel as you'd expect; his name's Ignatius. I guess in his case he's lucky someone *did* think to contract his name. Whoops, I'm —

'What sort of guy do you want?' Mae asks.

'Anyone genuine, loving, and someone who will accept me for who I am.'

'Yeah, the same for all of us.'

'But you're already emailing someone, aren't you?'

'Yeah, but there's ten times as many crackpots after me as well. You really have to be careful.'

Mae uploads my photos and profile to a website called *Find a Filipina*. There are about 200,000 girls on there, ranging in age from eighteen (as if they're *really* eighteen) to sixty-two. If I don't have anyone by the time I'm sixty-two, I'll give up. I suppose that's a bit harsh, because I have no idea of those ladies' circumstances. I shouldn't pre-judge; one of those poor women might be a widow after an unfortunate tragedy deprived her the love of a forty-year marriage; one's husband may have up and left after finding a younger woman, perhaps on *Find a Filipina*; or, God forgive me, they could be so dog ugly that they wouldn't have a chance of finding anyone even if they lived to *one hundred and sixty two*.

A pop-up flashes, "Profile Accepted". 'We'll come back tomorrow,' Mae enthuses.

We leave the café and trek back to my place. The temperature hovers around 28 degrees. It is 5.00 p.m. The evening descends, compressing everything into the streets of Balinad, on the outskirts of Cebu. Motorcycles race along the road, buzzing and screaming while others gurgle like a pond of croaking frogs. Another motorcycle chugs by, weighed down by a family of four. Two children straddle the gasoline tank, while the rider stands to allow sufficient room for nervous parents side-saddled behind him. They grip the underside of the seat, bracing themselves against the rigors of corrugated tarmac.

A swarm of tricycles flee a set of traffic lights as they attempt to catch the northward rolling cacophony. Billows of fumes hover and mix with black diesel pumped out of jeepneys, many of which have rarely seen a service centre since white flags waved an end to the Second World War.

The thick carbon monoxide blanket stretches its threads across the city, intermingling with industrial emissions and carcinogens exhaled by the cigarette dependant population of Cebu. Pedestrians hold handkerchiefs to their face; the Filipino Pollution Filter, that in all reality offers little to no benefit. Cars and trucks honk and toot, swerving and jockeying for prime positions on the congested road. Some young lads in a passing jeepney cheer and whistle. I flush deep crimson after I notice that Mae had playfully undone the lace of her yellow top – which I am wearing.

'Do you think anyone will message me?' I ask.

'You'll probably have a few tomorrow, but remember, the profile won't go online until it's approved by the webmaster.'

'Profile? Upload? Webmaster? All this stuff is so new to me. All I want is the chance to get a boyfriend.'

'Listen Cin. It'll work out. Just wait 'til tomorrow.'

I know I complained about people who shorten names. Mae once called me 'Jac' and I freaked. She quickly apologised and said, 'What can I call you then?'

I shot her a quizzical glance: 'What's wrong with Jacinta? It is my name.'

'Too big a mouthful,' she said. 'Think I'll call you Cin'.

I was angry and didn't want to accept it. The first few times I didn't even respond. Then it grew on me. Mae is my best friend and I don't want anything to jeopardise that. At times I feel like a Christian sinner. Anyone who hears me answer to Cin in the street or the mall looks at me with scornful eyes. *Ah, she must be on her way to church to confess.*

I remember reading about a king of England with the strange name of Edward the Confessor. In years far hence, I visualise huge banners strung across Makati and Manila, celebrating the inauguration of Jacinta the Sinner as the Philippines eighteenth president. Yeah, sure. What a blight that would be on my faith and on Catholicism in general.

We pass stands of tricycles, motorcycles and jeepneys vying for the seven peso, five minute uphill climb into Balinad. Close by, Gaisano's Country Mall dominates the shopping precinct, while nearby, the Spanish influenced Montebello Hotel hosts international visitors eager to experience the culture of the 7107 island archipelago.

We near my home in the small community of Apas. Much of its perimeter abuts a huge military base, one of hundreds in the Philippines. The main street is bordered by tiny shops and food stalls, a school, and a lawyer's office. The junction heading the street hosts a temporary emporium of vendors frying fish and prawns on warped steel plates and ancient griddles; some boil rice in huge colanders, and others roast chickens in clunky rotisseries. The enticing aromas compel me to buy a baked fish to take home as a surprise for mama.

A young girl touts mangoes from a dilapidated cardboard box. She probably purchased them earlier from a market stall and struggled to carry all twenty of them back home. She now sells them for five pesos profit, netting maybe, after discounts to friends and neighbours, ninety pesos for her afternoon's work. That might be the sum total of her family's daily income. Ninety pesos sounds a lot, until you reconcile that it would not fill two people in McDonald's. The bustling illegal markets continue to attract many, therefore justifying the trader's regular attendance.

Groups of locals congregate in friendship, gossiping and time-wasting. Most have no jobs or means to productively utilise their time. Young lads kick a football; others throw a basketball against a shop wall, and two ten-year-old boys practice rolling cigarettes. They probably started four years' earlier.

From the potholed main street radiate tiny lanes, barely wide enough to allow Mae and me to walk side by side. The lanes are ragged bare earth, hardened by the constant trampling of residents' comings and goings. A trench of discarded grey-water and slush from homes not connected to the sanitary system flows alongside. An iridescent green sludge accompanies the stream flowing from washing buckets and tubs. A kaleidoscope of colour competes with the odour.

Fences of corrugated iron, reclaimed concrete blocks, wire mesh and other impenetrable material, provide a barrier to potential burglars. The rickety habitats beyond are the pride of their owners, but fall far short of residential building codes. Construction is cheap and haphazard; buildings are pieced together with concrete blocks and iron sheets into which are fitted small louvre windows and plywood front and rear doors. The homes are generally assembled by family members and handymen and are constructed with no permanence in mind – as if their owners might need to disassemble them to relocate elsewhere in the middle of the night. And that night *will* arrive, for the land upon which these homes sit is land owned by the military. The homes' owners are illegally squatting on the land – as they have so done for nearly forty years.

Mae slots in behind me as the laneway narrows. We wave to neighbours who sit in doorways trying to escape the stuffiness of their homes. No one has air conditioners – a fan is a luxury. Dogs yap from three-square-metre front yards, cats scurry across fence tops, zeroing in on rats' whiskers twitching from behind drain pipes, cracked foundations and split black plastic garbage bags. Ninety-eight decibels of American Idol scream out of open windows: something about lights shining for you and all being yellow too. A bad version of Coldplay's original.

I push open our gate. The steel base screeches across the concrete path. I cringe. I should have lifted it. I chastise myself as I try to erase the memory of my teacher scraping her nails down our school blackboard. The distraction frees my mind and I wonder what it might be like if I were walking side by side with my new foreigner instead of Mae.

Never will I be embarrassed or ashamed of my environment, but when I imagine walking hand-in-hand along these smelly, third-world lanes, I think of wide roads, concrete footpaths and palm trees on the sidewalk as we see on nearly every Hollywood-produced movie and sitcom. Would Americans expect to see the same here? I hope not, because if so, they'd be extremely disappointed.

By the same token, I don't want anyone feeling sorry for me. I am who I am and I'm born into my environment just as a prince or princess is born into theirs. Luck of the draw, one might say. I just hope that whoever I do bring into my home is sympathetic to the ways of the world and that they realise that many make the best of what they've got – no matter what that might be.

Mama greets us at the doorway. An expectant look pinches her face. She speaks little English despite my having tried to tutor the basics. She gets by, picking up bits from American television. It was so different in her day. There was little use for the English language. It was spoken mainly by visiting American army personnel. Schools taught only our local language, Visayan in the provinces, and Cebuano in the city. They're essentially the same, but each has retained its own peculiar afflictions and accents. During mama's schooling, English was available only as an optional subject in college. Now, English is mandatory in all schools, and Cebuano has given way to the new 'Filipino' which is the politically correct name for Tagalog, the language spoken by nearly 80% of Filipinos.

'Hello mama. Here's Mae.'

'Kumusta sila si Jacinta ug Mae.'

'Hello mama Sequentez. We brought fish,' greets Mae as she hands over the plastic shopping bag.

Mama smiles and mumbles something about fish sweating in plastic. Mae and I climb the stairs to my room. 'Stairs' is a misnomer – they are more of a make-shift ladder, straight up and down. I'd prefer one of those brass fireman's poles, but climbing up would be beyond my physical capabilities.

My room is about three metres square. A flimsy curtain separates my brother's bedroom on one side and mama and papa's on the other. You can imagine I have next to no privacy. None of us snore. Thank goodness. It wouldn't matter if we did because next door's roosters are raucous enough to drown out a community's cheers for Manny Pacquiao winning yet another world title.

A calendar, folded over to August, hangs from a crooked nail on the wall. No dates are circled. Free. Actually, the whole year is free. Nothing of significance pending in my life. Maybe that's why I so desperately want a boyfriend; to reinstate the love that has long since escaped my parents – I am no longer the 'cuddly little thing' shown off to all and sundry at every opportunity. Now I want someone to love, to think about, to plan a future with. And it might happen soon, now that Mae is helping me.

My single bed has not re-made itself – I'm not always so lazy. A cluster of fluffy dolls, bears and a dog spill onto the floor as if someone had stolen an armful of cheap prizes from a circus sideshow and dumped them on my bed. My dressing table is one of dad's better inventions. He inverted a cardboard box and covered it with a white linen cloth. A small mirror hangs on the wall above. Great for doing my hair – crap for make-up.

Mae scans my wardrobe and selects two tops to borrow for the weekend. We are always exchanging clothes, although many of hers are too, what should I say, seductive? We spend the next hour talking about dating foreigners before descending to the lounge room to watch mid-afternoon television. Mae joins us for our dinner of *adobo,* a chicken dish prepared in soy and vinegar dressing. A huge bowl of rice takes centre stage. The baked fish waits on the sideboard. Papa will demolish it on arriving home from work.

My eldest brother, Jacob, walks Mae home. He is a token chaperone, a visible deterrent to anyone who might want to cause my friend harm. He's proved his worth by walking me home from school, but that is only to prevent any casual chatting up. In a dangerous situation I reckon he would just panic and run off in the opposite direction. I hope not.

I go to bed early to dream of guys viewing my profile and sending me love and kisses.

THREE

THE FOLLOWING MORNING I RISE at 6.30 a.m. to claim the first shower. It is always a quick run in, sponge-down, run out episode, because the tank holds only enough water for three showers. The water flows not from a proper hot water system but from a small tank wedged in the roof space. It holds a constant twenty-four degrees – courtesy of the high daytime temperatures – and gravity feeds the shower, laundry and kitchen.

My brothers shower at night, or at least they are expected to. Sometimes I think they have an affinity against cleanliness. Of course that is at odds with our Catholic upbringing which lectures that cleanliness is next to Godliness.

I wind a scarf around my wet hair, knowing the jeepney trip will blow it dry in time for school. I race into the kitchen and scoff a bowl of freshly-boiled rice and a piece of the previous evening's left over *adobo*. There is no sign of the baked fish.

I plonk the plate and bowl into the sink – mama will

later castigate me for it– grab my bag, and rush to a departing jeepney that will safely (I hope) deliver me to St Theresa's College in time for my eight o'clock class. I can't wait for this daily ritual to end. The school year will be over in three months; just two days shy of my eighteenth birthday. I have not yet decided about further study. I could go to university, but I really don't know what I want to do with my life. It seems pointless, and maybe counterproductive, to enrol in university (if papa could afford it) when I've no idea what course of study I should follow. I could spend six months studying a subject I'll later abandon. Of course there is always the possibility that a rich American might whisk me away before I even think of the future. Yeah, I wish.

I'm forever amazed how some girls, and boys too I suppose, decide at eight- or nine-years-of-age that they're going to be a doctor or lawyer or scientist. In the intervening years they either change direction or totally lose the plot, because some of them end up working in shops or driving taxis or climbing coconut palm scaffolds on building sites. They once spouted grandiose claims (perhaps instilled by their parents) only to later realise they can't, or won't, make the grade. Some give up all hope – *I'm just a dumb-ass*. Others frame a period of evaluation and resolve to accept second or third best, with the justification: *I couldn't stay in college, my parents needed my help.*

Yes. You're right. That *is* a total cop out. Surely, their parents would be far better rewarded, and proud, had their child endured the hard slog and graduated? Ultimately, parents reap the fruits of their children's success. Never have I heard anyone in my college say, 'I can't wait until I leave school so I can work in a shop,' or, 'I can't wait until I'm eighteen so I can make a major contribution to society as a janitor in McDonald's.'

I'm sure some parents are locked in the dark ages. They do not realise there is more opportunity in the present economic climate than ever before. They're unable to take a positive view and accept that Filipinos who want to work and achieve, can and will. Sure, some career paths might *seem* demeaning. Carers and maids top no one's list of career aspirations, BUT, there is a heavy demand for these roles, especially overseas – Dubai, Singapore and Hong Kong spring to mind. The pay is far more than the commensurate rate here in the Philippines. A few years' savings could set up a girl for life. For me though, I don't think I would go overseas just to clean someone's house. I do enough at home. Then again, I suppose if it were a big foreign mansion with TVs and stereos, huge mirrors and air conditioning, and soft leather couches that I could sink into, well, perhaps I could warm to the idea.

Males have similar opportunities. Take 'sailors' for instance. Private and commercial charters always welcome reliable Philippine seamen. And look how call centre opportunities have skyrocketed in recent years. The Philippines now boasts 1 million employed across the country's call centres, with Cebu claiming only 5% of those personnel.

Sure, I could follow many other girls' paths and study nursing. Numerous options spring from medical qualifications. Vacancies for nurses continue to escalate. It is a skill forever in demand, both as a career and as an immediate first-aider in cases of domestic or similar crisis. I've heard of many graduates accepting overseas positions that offer exceptional salaries compared to our depressed currency. The difference in economies and exchange rates between Philippines and most western and Middle East countries astounds me. I've heard of girls in their first year of nursing earning as much in a month as we would earn in a year at home – if we could actually get work. There is huge demand for Filipino nurses to relocate to America and Europe (including England) with similar opportunities available in Qatar and the United Arab Emirates.

———————

At lunch time I meet Mae at our usual table inside the school cafeteria. We move outside because the noise in the cafeteria wallows in a huge wave of talk, laughs, sniggers, cries, *maayong hapons*, jokes, chastisement, jealous rages, *makita ta ugmas*, excuse mes, see you laters, and a cacophony of other indecipherable babble. I ask Mae to wait for me after school so she can accompany me to the internet café. 'You'll need 20 pesos for an hour,' Mae whispers. That quietens me. I've been so swept up anticipating messages, I hadn't even thought of having to pay for the computer. I should have realised that they're not going to let me use it for free. I guess I am so overwhelmed about the forthcoming experience that I have lost my usual thought process. 'Can you lend me? I'll pay you back tomorrow after I get money from papa.' Mae is always good for a loan.

I text mama to advise that I'll be a bit late. She's used to my spending time with Mae.

A traditional afternoon downpour drowns out the old air raid siren signifying end of school. The premature rain season holds us to high alert in preparation for frequent typhoons which cause havoc to pedestrians, traffic and anyone without cover. Rain seeps through canvas awnings over fruit stalls; it trickles down the side of jeepney roofs and into the passenger compartment, where it joins the sideways rain blowing through the open windows which are only open because the owner cannot afford to pay for new glass or Perspex; and it falls through the roof at the back of our home and into buckets on the kitchen floor.

But that's not the worst of it. Mama tries to prepare our evening meal, dodging the obstacles like downhill skiers weaving through a slalom course. 'Jackson, when you fix hole in roof?' – I loosely translate. Papa utters his stock answer: 'Before the next storm, my dear.' I think there have been twelve storms and an extra two buckets since the hole first appeared. Maybe, I wonder, I should just save the 20 pesos I'm going to use at the 'net café to help dad buy new iron for the roof.

Nup. No way. Stupid idea.

We arrive at the café at 5.30 p.m. Soaked. Hair stinking like a wet dog. I hand over my P20, which Mae had given me only a few minutes earlier. That is part of our 'con-tract.' She won't just hand it to the cashier; she has to first pass it to me, specifically to authenticate that I've actually borrowed the money. She uses her first ten minutes to check email, opening five before concealing one from me. Mae doesn't hide much, but when it comes to boys, well, that's a different matter. She says and does things I have seen only in movies. And couple of those things were in movies I should never have seen.

That is one of the funnier sides of Mae. I have to tell you about it. She had invited me and a couple of our school friends to her home one Saturday afternoon to watch pirate movies. I imagined I'd be watching *Pirates of the Caribbean* because Johnny Depp is one of our favou-rite actors. On the other hand, I hoped to not have to sit through *Pirates of Penzance*, because we did a rendition of that in drama class at school. I hated all the 'heave ho me hearties' crap pirate talk.

We sprawled out on her couch, sneaked her dad's cheap cask of wine and a few bags of prawn crackers and sat before the screen. We were more interested in the movie than continuing small talk that we'd already covered, two or three times, at school. Mae slid in the DVD. The credits rolled, but waves didn't. Moments later I realised the title, *Pirates of Privates*, had nothing to do with piracy. Sometimes I think I must be thick or naïve, because it was only then that I grasped the true interpre-tation of 'pirate' movie.

Of course I watched it. We all did – out of respect,

naturally, for Mae's hospitality. We dazzled at the inter-twining flesh; the oohs, aahs and gasps; concentration, consummation, conjugation, copulation, ejaculation, lu-brication, masturbation and any other 'ation' the producer could encourage the aspiring F grade actors and actresses to perform. It certainly left nothing to my imagination. I chalked it up as a learning experience, and, goodness me, did I learn a lot. Had Mae's parents unexpectedly turned up, I have no doubt that I would have been subjected to a totally different learning experience. And so would have Mae.

She logs in to my profile. A box flashes onto the screen: 'You have five new messages.' I open the virtual envelope and quickly trash two welcomes from site administrators. Big deal. Next one?

'Mike' lives in Minnesota and has recently separated from his wife because of 'problems'. 'Seeking a lady to spice up my life and give me a reason for living.' He is forty-seven-years-old and looks sixty. He could well be, but I don't yet know how many profiles are botched with false dates of birth, false marital status and false life expe-riences. That doesn't worry me too much, because when you see someone's photo, you sort of know straight away if you're going to be compatible or not. Not that I'm expe-rienced at that, but I just reckon that when people say, 'It's what's on the inside that counts,' they're only half right. I reckon they've got everything back to front. You don't discover one's inside, until you get past first base of the initial meeting. If there's no visual attraction – that feeling of wanting to be with someone – you'll never see the inner being. It's like venturing into the unknown when sampling a new culinary delicacy. If it looks ghastly, you'll shove the plate away as far as possible – as well as utter a few unsavoury words. It could well be your best indulgence ever, but if you lack initial interest, you'll never know. On that basis I delete Mike.

As I did with Jim, and Geoffrey, although Geoffrey did catch my attention. *Recently finished university where I graduated in Commercial Law. Going to take two years off before I launch my own practice. Looking to start my life with the woman of my dreams. Interests: Bush walking, chess and oriental spiders.* Started well. But the interests? I've got no problem with trying to learn chess. I'm pretty good at Chinese chequers, so chess is just a variation of a theme. I can also take to the bush. I've never minded walking, although I trudge most of my kilometres along shopping malls and college aisles. But oriental spiders? What the heck's that all about? Am I supposed to walk into our living room and confront a glass case full of spiders? Dead or alive? Would they be pinned to black cardboard, like they do with butterflies, and exhibited behind a gold-embossed frame hanging on a feature wall of our home. I can just see myself: *Hi come in. Welcome to our home. Here's our wall of family snaps: weddings, great-uncles and aunts, the first grandchild, great ancestors, sporting moments, my first callisthenics concert and oh, by the way, you must look at my husband's collection of rare oriental spiders.* Yeah, that fits. I jab the delete button.

We head home. I am disappointed but equally consoled with the hope that tomorrow will bring a more wholesome inbox full of exciting applications from eligible guys across the world.

The next day my purse is bare so I do not attend the café. Mama had given me 20 pesos, which I reluctantly passed on to Mae. I'll wait until Saturday when I receive my P100 weekly allowance from papa. I won't risk spending twenty here and twenty there on what might turn out to be a fruitless chase, so I discipline myself to attend the 'net café only on Saturdays and Wednesdays.

I count down the hours. On Saturday I wake early and do my laundry before anyone stirs. I complete a few chores, not so much to help mama, but to score points from papa. My initiative might inspire him to slip me a few extra pesos. To boost the prospect, I make soup and rice and serve my parents breakfast in bed.

'That's nice,' papa says in appreciation.

'It's all right. I had some extra time after the laundry and sweeping.' I don't dare drop too many hints like the floor I've mopped and the previous evening's dishes I've washed and cleared from the sink. However, I do top it off by saying, 'Don't worry about the boys. I made extra rice and left it on the table.' Mama eyeballs me with her *I know what you're up to* look.

Papa spoons in a mouthful of rice as if performing a taste test. He offers no comment about the food, but casually mentions that if I go out before he rises, I can take P120 from his wallet. 'Go and have a good day,' he smiles.

I return a wider smile. 'Wow, thanks papa,' as if his gesture is an unexpected surprise. I leave the room accompanied by mama's glare: *You wouldn't get away with that with me.*

An hour later I waltz into Mae's home and drag her to the café. I don't really need her; I just feel more comfortable in her company. We enter shortly after opening. It's already crammed with teens because Saturday is one whole peak period. People bring along friends, as have I, rather than prop in front of the screen on their own. Some want to brag about conquests, about the 'great catch' they've secured; others wanted to brag about the 24,002 aliens they've killed on War of the Worlds; and a few studious kids sit with headphones, ignoring all around them while they research politics, medicine or breeding habits of the endangered Philippine Eagle.

The café's reputation for fewer line dropouts than their counterparts means that some patrons hold permanent bookings to guarantee access to their favourite computer. Others amble in at the same time on 'their' day of the week. I hand over P20 and proceed to number seven, a five year-old refurbished Dell obviously discarded by a government department because it still deploys the Philippines' government logo as a screen saver.

I brush a trail of crumbs from the desk and log in to my account. The message box flashes onto the screen, this time showing twenty-two messages. I scroll through, saving the better prospects (by name and nationality) till last while deleting others to save time and space.

The unfortunate rejects are guys riding on a free membership. I reason that if someone is serious about finding the right girl, they would at least subscribe to a membership to allow them added benefits of posting extra photos, chat facility and unlimited mail access – all of which enhance their prospects of finding the right life partner. Those I discard are blatantly after one thing – something I'm not offering – so I decide there's no point in wasting part of my hour replying to *them*.

Of the twenty-two, I cull the list to two contenders: Christopher and Wayne. Both have appealing photos. Christopher is from Vermont in the USA and Wayne hails from Devon in England. I'd handwritten a generic reply at home, so now I have only to transfer it to the computer: *Hi there. Thank you for taking your time to write. I am replying because I like your profile and your photo and your outlook on life. I joined this site because I want to find the love of my life. I'm not wanting to sound like a character from a fiction romance, but I've long preferred to find a person from the western world. Perhaps it's the way we're brought up here because we are largely influenced by Americans and American television. Even our English is Americanised. I am a person who prefers to be with just one man. I don't cheat or mess around behind your back and I am a person of simple needs. I am a homebody, but would easily adapt to any lifestyle. I would love to learn more about you and am willing to exchange much more about me. Hope to hear from you again. Jacinta.*

I interrupt Mae and show her the photos of Christopher and Wayne.

She glances over my shoulder. 'He's all right isn't he? Talk about tall, dark and handsome.'

'Which one? They're both tall!'

'Christopher, silly. Chris' and Cin. Got a ring to it, don't you think? You could have a child and Chris-Cin it. Get it? Christen?'

'Yeah, sure, M. I haven't even spoken to him and you've already got us having kids.'

I am disappointed at the rate my hour dissolves. I pledge to be more careful in future so I can spend more time on those who matter rather than read tales of those I wouldn't even share a bus seat with. I can't afford to pay extra and I can't rely on papa slinging me an extra twenty. So preoccupied am I about excess charges, I realise that I haven't advised Christopher and Wayne of my inability to reply before the following Wednesday.

Mae and I stand outside the café, comparing our activities of the previous hour. Talk dominates every idle moment, no matter where we are. We talk about anything. That's an indisputable female attribute. I talk about the two guys who've emailed and how good it would be if we could email more often. I guess there will be other messages filling the inbox by Wednesday, so I console myself that very shortly I'll be corresponding with a potential date.

I remember Mae telling me how she'd communicated with one guy for five months until she found out from a cousin that the very same guy was communicating with her also. I find that hard to believe, but I suppose if someone is seeking a particular type of person, it's highly probable they'd find similar traits in members of the same family. Deep inside, I suspect that Mae is corresponding with a guy who is cheating left, right and centre. Quite probably there are another half a dozen girls with whom he maintains contact.

I won't let that happen to me, although if it does, I guess I'll never even know. Guys are no different on the internet than in real life; most are out for all they can get. Maybe I sound harsh, but despite being three months shy of my eighteenth birthday, I've learnt enough about mendacious males to be wary, suspicious, distrusting and non-committal until *I* decide when *I* will accept them as worthy of my undivided attention. I'm sorry if I sound pompous or full of myself, but that's how I am.

FOUR

WEDNESDAY'S SCHOOL IS EXTREMELY TRAUMATIC. I can't concentrate. I daydream of sitting in the internet café, typing an epic to Christopher or Wayne. Or both. I've convinced myself that one of them is mine, and guess I lean toward Christopher after receiving Mae's approval of his profile. I pinch myself to reality several times during the day so I can jot down tutorial notes. I'll review the day's lessons at home.

When the final siren blasts me from class, I zip through a throng of dawdling teachers and students. My bag swings across my back like a grandfather clock's pendulum, and my hair trails behind like Zorro's black cloak. I arrive at the café in the same time Flo Jo won her 1988, steroid-assisted, 100 metre gold medal – just as happy and out of breath. I've left Mae far behind. I don't worry because she'll soon catch up if only to find out what happened with my guys.

I hand over another P20. The manager automatically assigns computer number seven. Mae sits next to me as I open twelve replies. I scroll through to my targets. I scan Christopher's response but as I read on, my interest drops. Sure, he has some good qualities, but I am tentative about a guy who commences his email: 'Hello to my darling new wife.'

Excuse me? That's way too eager and presumptuous, or is that just the American way? As I read on I learn how he looks forward to meals like his mother made, (he has her collection of recipe books for goodness sake); he likes going to his mother's favourite shops; and then to top it off, he wants to teach me to knit!

I'm open to doing anything, and knitting might be fun, even though I've never had a need or desire to knit. Besides, who wears wool in Cebu, and what girl would want to learn knitting from a guy? It would be like a guy conducting pre-natal classes – some things are solely a woman's domain. I dispatch Christopher's profile to Bill Gates' hallowed trash can where he can forge a friendship with Geoffrey and his creepy oriental spiders.

I move on to Wayne. What a contrast. I consider the difference between the two guys, and wonder if there is a vast cultural canyon between Britain and America. Wayne starts his reply so eloquently, and it just goes on and on, extending to nearly four pages. I credit him with making an effort because I'm sure he wouldn't have done this with every girl, though I do accept the possibility exists; he might have used the same message and personalised it each time. But why bother if you're serious? That's one of the internet's problems. One can read something, but it might not necessarily be true. I've spoken of people being duped and scammed, but there is also a hell of a lot of personal deceit – and the male is not always the perpetrator.

Wayne lives in the south of England. That doesn't mean much to me because I know nothing about England other than its cold climate. Very cold. I've learnt a little of English royalty: Henry VIII and his six wives, the long-serving Queen Elizabeth II, and Prince Charles' late wife Diana, Princess of Wales.

Wayne opens himself like an encyclopaedia. Full of facts. He works as a home handyman. We call that an 'odd jobs person' so I don't know if it's much of a trade. Maybe he just cuts lawns and changes light bulbs for old ladies. I don't know, but I suppose I'll learn a lot more later on because he plans to start his own business. He's very appealing in his photo; has a physique built on college football. I try hard to grasp his explanation of the distinction between various games and codes. I don't know much about male sport, but I do know that a keen sportsman is probably a good catch because it means they're interested in healthy pursuits. It also means they probably don't smoke. A glance further down his profile confirms my theory. 'Non-smoker'.

He is separated from his wife – or so he says – and in the final stages of divorce. The second one. That doesn't faze me; I already know about western society's throwaway marriages and the fact that wedding vows are honoured only until the end of the service. After that they become severable by mutual consent or for other reasons like adultery – the final straw that separates couples, or *one* of the couple, who had judiciously heeded the promise to love, honour and obey.

But wait. He's been married twice? I have to wonder why. Does he get bored with life? Has he played around and been sprung by his wife? I scrawl a note to raise the matter later on. It will be delicate, because I don't want to sound as if I'm subjecting him to a full-blown military interrogation. Nah, forget it. He isn't my only hope. I have an inbox full of prospective boyfriends. I'd feel as if I'm unwrapping a new gift from second-hand paper. Anyone who's been married is seen as 'used goods' if you know what I mean. Think matrimonial recycling program. Does nothing for the carbon footprint, but does leave surplus new goods on the shelf. eBay might even announce a classification for used partners and second-hand spouses: *Bid now! Closing in 38 hours. Or, Buy It Now for only $200. See item description. Will deliver – contact seller for details. No International Postage.*

This future model should not be rejected. As international conferences and movements collaborate to reduce carbon footprints and promote recyclable energy – and promote recycling in general judging by western society's plethora of kerbside recycling bins – we will hear delegates propose the new initiative: 'Spouse recycling depots.' If 'depots' sounds too industrial, an injection of 'political correctness' will conceive Spouse Recycling Studios: Just drop off your partner, pay a token carbon tax, (surcharge for blondes because of their inefficient oxygen handling capacity) and leave with a clear conscience that you're shaping a better world.

But some won't leave the premises. They'll linger, glance over their shoulders to ensure no one's looking, and then proceed through an adjacent door, scan a few rows of Surplus Spouses, and presto, they'll hook up with a recently discarded model, walk him or her to an appropriate 'make-over' facility, pay another fee to remove the statutory 'Recycled' sticker from the product's forehead (at that juncture receiving a credit for the aforementioned deposited partner) after which they'll race home eager to test the 'sustainability' of their new product, because everything politically correct must be *sustainable*.

The transaction will be covered by purchaser protection, statutory warranties and extended warranties (capped at five years) – a win / win situation for all.

Yeah, that's the future of recycling.

But back to Wayne: I can't see us starting on equal footing – two souls uniting under different circumstances. When we come to explore intimacy, our expectations will be unequal. I'll wonder if he's thinking about his previous wife, or wives. I'll be so scared that if I don't make him happy, well, he might just return to his former domain. To be fair, the one thing I have learned in church is to not judge others. There is only one who can do that, and I will leave that to Him.

Wayne, on the other hand, will think he's so lucky to have scored a young woman. He'll conjure a view of me draped around his neck like human bling. All well and good I suppose – until I tarnish with age.

I see myself as do many Philippine girls from young teens to early twenties, on the arm of a guy who appears far beyond retirement age. The image always frightens me: how do we interact with a partner so *old*? We often defend that age is just a number, a worthless figure that identifies one's time on this planet. I've since learnt that vast age differences are frowned upon in western society, but really, what is the problem? What harm is caused if a couple – say, twenty years apart in age – reward each other with a true bond; a cohesiveness that some put down to being 'made for each other'; a unity that is founded and preserved with true and pure love – the compassion to do anything for each other, to love and trust and to accept all the wonderful qualities and little idiosyncrasies of their partner? The outsiders don't see our compatibilities and share our feelings. Perhaps for us, whether Filipino, Thai or Korean, we do fall for the inner being rather than the superficial exterior. Besides, who set standards that one should partner or marry those only within a specific age bracket? If I fall for a guy 30 years my senior, what concern is it of anyone else's? Perhaps we seek a level of maturity we cannot find within our own circles. I've posed the question: *Would I marry a 50-year-old Filipino?* I look at it this way: If I dismiss a person because of his age, I could deprive myself a lifetime of love and happiness. Even though it's hard to deal with rhetoric, I sincerely believe that I would marry him – if he could offer all that I want.

And there you have it. I just admitted my material-istic desire and want for a better and more fulfilled life. Perhaps, subconsciously, there *is* a trade-off. Access to material wealth at the expense of flouting society's expec-tations. But I know that in my heart, if I truly love a man, it will not matter whether he drives a Bentley or rides a bicycle. My little verse conflicts with mama's: *If there's no food on the table, there's no love in the heart.*

I whisk through the other eighteen replies, discard twelve no-hopers and to the other six I send a thanks-for-your-interest-I'll-be-in-touch-shortly message. I know it is cruel to keep them on a string but I have only 20 minutes left to reply to Wayne.

Mae remains at her computer, welded to a chat line. I learn that is much easier than emailing to and fro, but I'll save that for later. I believe if someone is prepared to devote time to writing letters and emails rather than take the easy way out by sitting on the end of a phone, their intentions must be serious.

I send another two pages to Wayne, telling him of my aspirations for life, how my parents accept the prospect of my leaving home to move to another country, how I am willing to accept his being twice married, and that I am interested in continuing contact.

Despite initial reservations, we fall into a twice weekly email routine. Wayne sends a couple of letters packed with photos of his home and general locale and we share phone calls that whistle and crackle as if our respective governments are sending encrypted messages within our transmission. We exchange frequent texts, a custom I soon curtail because international texts are so expensive – compared to domestic charges. As our friendship progresses we speak of meeting during his holidays. It would be an exciting progression from our Saturday mornings on Yahoo! Messenger and Skype. The vast oceans are about to be bridged.

I cherish the moment when Wayne said how much he wanted to meet me. I had been hoping and even expecting it to happen. It is natural when two people live in close proximity – but on the other side of the world? Totally different story. An unfamiliar wave of emotion gushed through me as he uttered the words: 'Jacinta, I want to see you and be with you. I think I should come over. I'll book a hotel and we can be together for a couple of weeks. I can meet your parents and you can show me around. What do you think?'

Of course I thought it would be great. But I didn't want my enthusiasm to sound like a dead giveaway. I quietly replied: 'That'd be nice.'

In reality, I could hardly wait. We made tentative arrangements for Christmas, which left me to deal with five weeks of nervous anticipation. I wondered whether this whole idea of Mae's would yield me the reward I hoped for. And I wondered if Mae had also been so lucky.

Time dissolves and evaporates all talk of arrival dates. Wayne tells me of problems renewing his passport and how his workload has dramatically increased in recent months. I have mixed feelings. While I am happy that he is gainfully employed, I am dismayed that I might not see him. I've already told mama and papa, and, of course, Mae.

I'm also embarrassed to add that in the back of my mind I wonder if I have been played for a fool. A temporary conversational toy? A friendly voice to placate him for a few precious minutes? Perhaps he even hopes I could rake together enough money to fly over to see him? But then again, if he thinks that, he obviously doesn't know the Philippines.

The next week my worst fears come true when Wayne phones and apologises for not being able to arrive in time for Christmas. He lays the blame squarely with the passport office. Whether or not that is true, I couldn't be sure. I guess I shouldn't speculate about whether or not he is telling the truth. In short, I don't think obtaining or renewing a passport is a big deal, but when I consider the complexities of our own National Statistics Office, I decide to afford him the benefit of doubt.

I am really dejected. I honestly wonder if my dream of meeting a foreigner will ever come true. I'm not at ease with his motives; I revisit my thoughts of him being just another scammer. Maybe everything he's told me has been one long tale infused with enough tension to keep me on the boil. But then again, I wonder, for what purpose? What would be in it for him? I certainly haven't been putting out in the chat room.

I withdraw from Mae and I withdraw from my parents. I stay in my room, shedding tears and suppressing anger, all the time scolding myself for having spent – wasted maybe – hundreds of pesos in my quest to find love. Why has no one ever told me that seeking love is so challenging and heartbreaking? Perhaps I read too much into things. Over react maybe? Is our friendship too fresh for me to establish a strong foundation of trust?

All progresses well when our communication increases with the closing festive season. He sends money for Christmas, although it doesn't buy much. I'm not an ungrateful person, but I learn that a foreigner sees hundreds of pesos as equal value to hundreds of pounds or hundreds of dollars. They have no concept of exchange rates and the value of our currency in the western market. Wayne sent me P200, thinking he's done me a great favour by giving me enough for Christmas with some left over for the New Year. Had he have sent £200.00 or even $200.00, *then* I would have enjoyed a prosperous Christmas and New Year.

The completed school year gives me ample free time to, rightly or wrongly – okay, wrongly – communicate with a couple of new guys. I don't consider it a payback, but the proposed Christmas visit fiasco sent my concerns soaring: had Wayne been perfectly honest with me?

This brings about a chance opportunity to meet David, an American, who texts that he'll be in the area. Maybe it's not such a 'chance' opportunity. We've exchanged a few emails, so now, when I really think about it, I haven't exactly been exclusive to Wayne. I justify my actions as 'returning friendship to the Americans.' The qualification here is that one who extends friendships on a dating site always harbours an ulterior motive. The future.

And then I wonder about the 'coincidence' of David just happening to be 'in the area'. The outskirts of Cebu are far from recognised tourist hotspots; to the contrary, the main drag reflects elements that would likely repel western vacationers. I qualify that by stating that I don't pour disrespect over my heritage and community. The areas of which I speak are far from affluent. They comprise crisscrossed lanes of unemployed and low income earners, as well as those who aspire for a higher standard of living but don't 'get the breaks' they expect from prospective employers or the government.

Consequently, these residential areas accurately reflect the Philippine economic climate of the disadvantaged. It is no secret that the Philippines does find plentiful resources from which to reward its top politicians and government advisors. It is in those areas of prestigious buildings and homes that tourists flock. Consequently, tourists spend money in those locations, and in so doing, perpetuate the cycle.

Putting that aside, we have great shopping malls: Ayala and SM; we have many historic churches and cathedrals; we have wonderful provincial beaches, and we have nearby islands that offer rich flora and fauna and underwater delights.

Alarm bells ring. Unless David does have local business interests, I must be sceptical about his just *happening* to be in the area.

When the day arrives, I am not totally surprised to see him. I am just disappointed that David is here and Wayne isn't. Nevertheless, I make time for him and invite him to my family's home after he brashly invites himself. The clincher is that he insists on treating us to dinner. How could I refuse? He arrives with folded arms, upon which totter pizzas, bottles of Coke, beer for my papa, chocolates for mama and a new top *and* a bunch of roses for me. I can see that David wants to make a move on my whole family. My brothers leech onto him with questions about basketball, American cars and the eligibility criteria to obtain America's Green Card.

I have warmish feelings for him. I don't think I'd get to the boil. Wayne hankers in the back of my mind.

I enjoy time with David, although I sense that he, too, is seeing others behind my back. That is way out of bounds as far as I am concerned. I want nothing to do with anyone who compromises on monogamy.

I guess I've breached my own standards.

FIVE

EARLY IN THE NEW YEAR my dreams mould into reality when Wayne reveals that he's booked the flight. The date of his expected arrival is February the fourteenth. Everyone knows the significance of February the fourteenth: Valentine's Day. I can't contain my excitement. I'm crushed by guilt for doubting him over the previous two months. Worse still, I carry the burden of having seen – and kissed – Dave. Why in God's name did I do *that?* I collect my thoughts and focus on Wayne as my future.

I run straight to Mae's house and barge through the front door, ignoring her mama and table of visitors. 'Mae,' I shout. 'He's coming.'

Everyone looks at me as if I've fallen into the safety of their home to escape a fictitious pursuer. Mae bounces from her room. Calms her parents: 'Cin's all right. She's just had some good news.'

Mae grabs my arm and yanks me into her room. 'When? You look so happy.'

'Of course I'm happy. This is the best news I've ever

had. I was really thinking this would never happen and that I'd wasted all those months emailing and texting. Now I know that it was all worthwhile.'

'All right, all right. When's he arriving?'

'Three weeks, one day, and sixteen hours. February fourteenth.'

'Valentine's Day?'

'Yeah. Wicked. He even selected the right day to prove how much he loves me.'

'Be careful, Cin. You don't know yet if he's really the one for you.'

'He is, Mae. I just know.'

Of course I don't really know. I am just using the power of positive thinking. Emotion grips me. Only two weeks earlier I'd kissed Dave in the hope that something wonderful might transpire. I didn't go racing round to Mae's because I wasn't sure how she'd react, although I did suspect she would pacify me with her: 'How will you know if you don't try samples?'

I can always rely on Mae to provide logical explanations. But "samples"?

I query her analogy and she justifies it with shopping. Trust her to explain something in terms I can comprehend.

'Just imagine you're looking for a special occasion dress,' Mae starts. 'You're not going to grab the first one off the rack; you're going to look around, try a few on, ignore the sales assistant's shrieks of: 'that looks good on you' (as do the other ten outfits) and then make a selection based on all the information you've gathered. It's exactly the same with dating. You can't just go out for the evening, kiss a guy, and then say: 'Marry me. I want to be with you for the rest of my life.'

I glare at Mae. Sometimes she makes more sense than my school teachers. She's what they call 'wise beyond her years'.

'I know you're right, Mae, but sometimes you trivialise things too much. There are times when we want to be sure that the dress will still be right in 20 years and that any little dresses will be cared for and not just left in a wardrobe to their own devices.'

Mae shoots me a quizzical look as if *I'd* lost it. I definitely won that one.

The next day I receive an email of Wayne's itinerary. He will arrive at Mactan Airport in the late afternoon, and then transfer by shuttle to the Montebello Hotel – the huge Spanish hacienda I mentioned that spreads behind Gaisano Country Mall. We'd spoken about hotels and accommodation, but I never thought he'd stay in a place like Montebello, not that *I'd* ever been there. Not inside, anyway. I had inquisitively looked in from the outside, but saw very little because it's one of those establishments protected by a throng of security sentries. I know foreigners stay there because I see them shopping in the mall, walking lop-sided with heavy bags, fingers straining against the lacerating handles while they struggle to the taxi rank. While we squeeze into cramped jeepneys, or straddle tricycles and motorcycles, the foreigners command taxis for even the shortest journey. They relish the comfort, the air conditioning and perhaps the pomposity of showing that they are a class above us.

Of course some of us use taxis occasionally, but the fare equates to about 50 jeepney trips. Where's the economic logic in that? Over the past year I've hailed only two taxis; one to take my *lola* to hospital and the other to escape being drenched by a sudden typhonic downpour.

The eve of the big day arrives. I busy myself with extra homework and domestic chores. I see Mae for an hour or so, but to be honest, I am growing tired of her quizzing me about what we are going to do, where we will go, what I would do if he actually proposes, and how far would I go with him. I snap a vague 'I don't know, I'm not sure,' to each of the four questions.

She turns on me: 'You shit me Jacinta. I did this for you, to get this Wayne guy, and now you treat me as if I'm a low-life prying into your secret business.'

I feel ill for having fobbed off my best friend. She's put me in my place. Mae's friendship means more to me than anything in the world – even any prospective relationship or marriage. I grab her and hold her tight. Tears fall to her shoulder. 'You're right, Mae. I'm so sorry. Maybe I'm selfish, I don't know. I love you for everything and for the person you are. I should tell you everything, and you know what? I really don't mind telling you, and I probably will. I'm just so nervous about the forthcoming two weeks. What if it doesn't work out? I don't want to think negative, but I don't even sleep some nights for fear of this not working. I know you'll say that there's plenty more fish in the sea and that sort of stuff, and I know you'd be right. Maybe it's the thought of failure, a premonition of insecurity or of not being in control? I don't really know, but what I do know is that I'm sorry for hurting your feelings and being a bitch.'

'Gee, Cin. You sure are worked up. Is there anything I can do?'

'Nah. It's all up to me, isn't it? Perhaps I just need some time alone to prepare.'

Mae leaves, a little despondent, but also a lot wiser because she's learnt more about me in ten minutes than she'd learnt in the previous five years. She now knows that I have a dependency weakness.

I withdraw into myself and retreat to my room doing essential girly things: painting toenails and fingernails, putting a bit of curl and bounce into my hair and plucking eyebrows. I also venture to other bits of personal plucking if you know what I mean – I don't go in for that waxing stuff.

Happy with my appearance and convinced that Wayne will surely notice my efforts of meticulous preparation, I offer to help mama tidy the house – or what tidying awaits in the sparsely furnished home. After that, I help prepare dinner – without a word spoken between us – and then watch TV for an hour before retiring to my room. I plan to get plenty of sleep, not because I am tired, but because a collection of grey bags stacked beneath my eyes need some serious remedial work. I know I won't sleep. I am too excited.

I flop into my sagging mattress and fight negative thoughts dangling before me. The first is that he won't arrive. I snap out of that and visualise myself standing in the Arrivals Lounge for three lonely hours before the plane's arrival. A staff member approaches and asks if I am okay. I respond in the affirmative and wait in hope at the gate for my dream man to rush into my open arms, replicating one of those slow motion movie scenes where the girl runs along the causeway, silk scarf flowing in the breeze, skirts and petticoats billowing and dancing like a sea of anemones waltzing to the tune of tropical tides, eyes fixed upon each other's, and lips suffused in preparation for the first kiss – the kiss that could seal the expectations and dreams of a lifetime.

I moisten my lips, ready to sigh at his soft touch, and imagine him lying next to me, tracing his fingers across my breasts and teasing my belly button. I haven't been with a boy in *that* way before and I am sure I'll be so nervous when the time comes. I feel the warmth of my inner glow, the pulsing tingles electrifying my core. I really want to wind up the voltage; to create sparks before my eyes, to transmit electrifying surges to every nerve-ending, but then I remember that I am not alone in the house. I flick the switch to reality and tug on the curtain of sleep.

Just as I am about to doze off, another thought drops before my eyes; one that might be worse than the prospect of him not arriving. What if he's ugly and nothing like his photos? What if he's used one of those Photoshop programs to enhance his manly status? Paint over a couple of wrinkles here, remove a hint of shaving rash there, colour a few strands of gray hair, and then, for the finishing touch, whiten the teeth.

It's no issue that I've given it a try. Well, not exactly me. Mae told me it would be a good idea to 'tweak' my photo a little. 'It won't do any harm,' she said as I watched her manipulate the computer screen with an arrow that grabbed my breast and stretched the image a few millimetres. 'Wow,' I said. I never knew about such things. I've heard of models being airbrushed and enhanced, but to be able to totally alter one's image is incredible. People could really be deceived by that. I didn't want to do it. I prefer to attract someone by my own appearance and merit – not by an artificial mock-up or simile. So I had Mae restore me to my former self. Or close enough to it.

So what will I do if Wayne is not as I expect? Will I simply excuse myself to the toilet and sneak out without him noticing? Should I be up front and splutter: 'I don't think it's going to work out'? Or will I just stay with him for the duration of his stay, appease him, accept lashings of gifts, tolerate his company – no matter how good or bad – and in the end just put it down to another life experience? That would be Mae's advice, and I know some girls who have done exactly that. They've just used up the guy for a few days or weeks to enjoy a no-expenses-spared holiday. I think a couple of them enthusiastically 'put out' for their supposed beloved to falsely confirm that a relationship did actually exist between them.

Sorry about the clichés. I live by them. So let me coin an old one from the sisterhood: 'A girl's gotta do what a girl's gotta do.' To each their own. It's not my place to pass comment. Let's just encompass all under the temptation of the apple. What girl can resist being treated like a princess for a week or so? Perhaps an introduction to intimacy would enhance the experience, but for me, the concluding emotional crash would be too much to bear.

Taking all that into account and showing compassion for the guy who had spent a substantial amount on fares and accommodation, I think I'd be frank and up front. Perhaps I should prepare myself with a spiel, just in case: 'I don't think we're compatible, but if you like I'll stay with you for the rest of your stay and show you around. I will introduce you to some family members, not like an introduction agency, but you know, something might click somewhere.'

Yeah, that's what I'll do. I write it down straight away because I'm often deceived by my memory. There was once a time in school where I'd formulated a great answer to a test question. I had all the fancy words and logic and pledged to write it in my subject book. Of course you know what happened. I picked up the book and searched my memory: *What was I going to write in here?* I stumbled over it for hours, got fairly close, but never could I re-cover, word for word, the absolute literary genius that now lies dormant within me, accompanying all the other lost words and solutions I'd sacrificed to the God of sleep and laziness.

Speaking of God, it is an ungodly hour of the night when I eventually fall into sleep's cavern.

At 6.30 on the morning of Wayne's arrival, I jump out of bed, panicking as if it is mid-afternoon and that I've missed his grand entrance. The roosters' crows signify otherwise. I scoff breakfast and shower, making sure I allow ample time to apply make-up. Alright. Time isn't really a problem. I have all morning and half of the afternoon. Wayne isn't due to arrive until 5.40 p.m. I am just impatient, nervous and over-anxious. Everyone knows that a girl's preparation is not a simple process.

I sometimes wonder what it would be like to be a Caucasian with the ability to be able to change my complexion at will, to whatever shade I desire, simply by dabbing a blusher across my cheeks. Strange, isn't it? In contrast, white women envy us because of our natural toned skin and a complexion that doesn't crease or wrinkle with age.

I tumble downstairs for lunch and am surprised to see my aunty in the kitchen probing mama about Wayne. Mama could tell her plenty – had she been interested. Instead, she tells Aunt Tracey that Jacinta's very happy and this modern dating thing has made her unusually radiant. A few days earlier I asked Tracey to accompany me to the airport as a mock chaperone, just in case I need help. Not that I feel in danger, but stories prevail of untoward events happening at airports; people-smuggling, bag snatches and recruiting drives for drug couriers. I guess I just don't want to take risks.

Aunt Tracey tells me how nice I look and that I'd better have a puff of oxygen because I am flushed in the face and breathing rapidly. Of course I am. I'm surprised that I'm not hyperventilating. This is a big step for me. There are only so many girls favoured by foreigners, so I am proud to be one of them. I am delighted that a man from the other side of the world has expressed interest in me, while most in my home town rarely cast me a second glance.

There are many benefits to marrying a foreigner, not the least of which are financial. I know people spout clichés like, 'Money doesn't buy happiness.' My response is that it certainly helps. There is a standard of living a foreigner enjoys that we could never experience in our home country.

They have huge homes (by our standard) with baths, showers, 2 toilets in most homes, large carpeted rooms and plenty of them, all manner of electrical appliances, air conditioning and proper heating, gardens with swimming pools and pantries crammed with food. And, there are jobs for everyone who wants to work. Yes, everything is much more expensive than in the Philippines, but much of that is due to our depressed economy. On the positive side, when we visit the Philippines our international currency buys so much more.

I could follow others and sit in bars frequented by affluent society. I could hope for a rich Filipino company director or politician to sweep me off my feet and promise me the world. Perhaps that's as contrived as searching for love on the internet. I don't know. It just seems so artificial, like they're selecting a puppy or kitten from a pet shop.

I'm not after diamonds and limousines. All I want is comfort. More than anything else I want love and kindness and a person prepared to devote his all to me as I will to him. *Am* I artificial? *Are* my expectations unreasonable?

Yes, I am pretentious and snooty. No, I'm not trapped in a class above myself or anything like that; I'm just particular about what I want from life. I want more than a Philippine husband could offer. Once again, I'm not criticising my fellow countrymen. I love my nationality and I love my country. May God bless them both. What I am trying to say is that I want more than to be left in a shanty town during the day while my husband drives a tricycle or taxi, or works in a factory for upwards of 16 hours a day, comes home tired and never gets to see me except for breakfast and an evening snack before going to bed. I know of such existences – the women accept their life's station, but have not one ounce of joy. Many know no better. They simply accept their given lifestyle. But not me.

———————————

I have no idea that in twelve months' time, I will encounter this exact scenario – to the letter.

SIX

I ARRIVE AT THE AIRPORT amid the eclipse of present and future. The following hour will determine my destiny. That is for certain. If Wayne *is* 'the one' my life will change for the better. If he is not, well, I'll feel sad for a short time and then head straight back to *Find a Filipina.com*.

As the seconds flash beside 5.40 p.m. on my oversize Mickey Mouse watch, so does my heart rate escalate to 160. It has not soared so high since I exhausted myself performing repetitive tumbles at school calisthenics – or on the day I panted over Mae's pirate DVDs.

I study the arrivals board. Bright LEDs flash: *BA 45 ex London, Heathrow, arriving now. Gate 4.*

Heart rate: 180.

Aunt Tracey lags behind as I rush to the arrivals foyer. I know there'll be a long wait while passengers surge through immigration and customs. Like an albino in the hundreds of passengers and staff in the terminal, I spot him right away. Not only because he is taller than most Filipinos, but because over previous months I'd imprinted him on my mind, each grain and pore of his features stencilled beneath my eyelids. Every day I studied his image – an artist's work in progress – until it became a reality; a cloned Wayne living within me. Okay. I sound like a freak. Maybe I am obsessed, but this is such a huge turning-point in my life.

He surveys the foyer perimeter, suitcase and bag in one hand and a spray of flowers in the other, feebly concealed behind his back. He looks questioningly at overhead signs which direct 'aliens' through two separate check-points and nationals through ten. The avalanche progresses smoothly, carrying Wayne through the barriers unscathed. We lock on to each other's eyes like lasers pinpointing a target. Our simultaneous smiles signify recognition. We step toward each other, happiness igniting our faces: a cautious smirk, a broad grin, then the mouth-stretching smile that spins the row of cherries on the poker machine, setting in motion bells and whistles signifying to all that the jackpot has been struck.

Heart rate: 195.

He is everything I imagined and better. *Gwapo*. He walks with a confidant air. A slight swagger sets him apart from other tourists. I look dreamily into his green eyes. They are not especially striking, but as one who lives in a country where eyes are every shade of dark brown, I feel as if I could gaze into them all day. And night.

Heart rate: 205.

We do not re-enact the movie scene I've previously described. Instead, we continue toward each other, as if electrically charged by magnetic poles, eyes for only each other, totally oblivious to the surroundings, moistening lips in preparation for the first kiss – which I hope will be a kiss of wonder, of splendour, of forthcoming pleasure, and of warmth and familiarity. The amalgamation of happiness, adrenalin and endorphins propel us together.

Heart rate: 220.

Moments later I shiver with disappointment. He proffers a cursory peck upon my cheek in the same manner he'd kiss his grandma on Thanksgiving. I make an allowance, feeling that he might be embarrassed by Tracey's watchful eye. It should be quite clear that Tracey is accompanying me, so either he is uneasy about displaying emotion in public, or he feels that I distrust him. Of course I don't; Tracey is good company and a token protective shield. No woman travels alone to strange places, even in the Philippines, where the congestion of eighty million people should guarantee that every person is safe every minute of the day. But that is the ideal world. Numerous muggings, fights, stabbings and abductions continue to be committed in broad daylight, right under people's noses.

There is also the prospect I refuse to consider: I do not meet his expectations.

So my very first task will be to erode his initial despondency and unearth a positive attitude about my present situation. I am amazed that we both wear blue jeans and burgundy shirts. That must be an omen of compatibility, although the less scatterbrained would discard it as coincidence. But coincidences do foster harmony, love and life's essence. I run my selection of tops and T-shirts through my mind. Aside from the formal whites and blacks, I have probably every other colour currently in fashion, and a few out of fashion – not to mention my unrestricted access to Mae's collection. I admit to keeping a couple that I'd borrowed and not returned to aunties and cousins, but the fact remains: from every colour available, we independently dressed the same.

There is no reason or desire to hang about the airport. Wayne suggests we have coffee, but I whisper that I've had my fill of airports after having been there for an hour. From that, he probably thought I was crazy, so I explain that I so feared being late that I chose to arrive early.

We hail a taxi and head straight for the Montebello Hotel. Tracey does the right thing and sits in the front like a former president, head rigid, looking forward. Not even a sideways glance to see what we might be up to in the back seat. I think she believes that three's a crowd. Perhaps her grace helps Wayne feel more at ease because he seizes the opportunity to clasp my hand as if it has belonged to him for years. I hope it will.

As we battle the early evening traffic I accept the journey for what it is – a jerky crawl along roads that are supposed to flow traffic with ease from point to point. And they once did, in the 1950s and 60s until our population exploded out of control while the country's infrastructure remained static and unimproved since the days of horses and drays and Spanish rule.

I bask in the gaze of adjacent drivers, passengers and

pedestrians, all jealous – or furious – of my snaring a foreign prize. Their expressions discharge the contemptuous judgements we're subjected to when dating outside our own race. Above their heads float cartoonists' speech clouds: *What's wrong with our boys?* I am immune to all that, thanks to my carapace of stubbornness. I am accepted within my own circle of family and friends for who I am and how I choose my company. I nestle proudly into Wayne and assure him the glares transmit best wishes.

He cranes his neck from side to side, taking in first impressions of Cebu's architecture, shanties and advertising hoardings. He reminds me of the sideshow attraction where a clown's head swivels from left to right inviting you to roll a ping pong ball down a chute and straight into the clown's gaping mouth.

'All the signs are in English,' he exclaims.

'Of course they are. We do speak English,' I reply with a little too much sarcasm.

'I know Jac. I suppose I expected signage to be in your own lingo, like the cities of Tokyo and Beijing we see on TV. Then again I don't really know what I expected.'

Heck. I have a problem already. I can understand that he might be ignorant of our over-use of American language. I can educate him very quickly about our history. But how do I educate him about my abhorrence of being called 'Jac'? I could lose him over this. Not ten minutes from the airport and already I have an issue. Should I just put up with it? After all, it is *only* a name. No! Why should

I compromise? If I compromise now I'll be compromising for the rest of my life. Here goes… 'Wayne. Since I was a small girl people have called me Jac. I hate it. It's one of those things that really niggles me; I'm sorry to bring it up when you've been here only ten minutes, but I'm so, so sensitive to it.'

He squeezes my hand so tight that I think it will graft to his. 'I'm sorry. The last thing I want to do is upset or hurt you. I'll never do that, so you can feel safe that I'll never call you Jac again. Jac.'

That makes me feel much better and his little smart-alec quip at the end shows me that he is a real person, with an underlying facetious streak maybe, but he shows no pretentiousness or superficial behaviour – he presents himself exactly as he is.

We walk hand-in-hand to Montebello's reception where Wayne settles the booking. A receptionist throws me a sideways glance, perhaps wondering what I'm do-ing with a guy who's just paid for a *single* suite. I blush, hoping that she doesn't think of me as a paid escort or bar girl. I drop my eyes – which is probably the worst thing to do in the circumstances – and thread my hand through Wayne's arm. Knowing I'll pass this desk many times, day and night, over the next fortnight, I do my best to show that we are in a genuine, committed relationship.

I am surprised at the size of the suite. Of course I have no concept of the interior of the hotel, nor that most suites are of a similar size with both a double and a single bed, comfortable easy chairs, nice table and writing desk, cable television, separate bathroom with bath and shower and spacious wardrobes complete with extra blankets that I am certain no one will *ever* use.

We fold into a quick cuddle of the type enjoyed by students at a twenty-year reunion; a Mediterranean hug, a kiss to each cheek, no romance, and no heart shattering eruptions of volcanic activity sending communities scattering for their lives. I am in heaven just feeling his arm wrapped around me. It is like winning a marathon – not that I've ever run one – and relishing the elation of breaking through the ribbon. I can't wait for the presentation. Sure, a hug is just a hug, but I recognise its significance as the commencement of a new era; a positive step forward into the world of love and romance, and, with an inkling of there being more to come.

I'm glued to the floor, like a century old statue, waiting for him to plant another on me, another faint kiss that will set my inhibitions free so I can tell him with my lips that he is the one. I sense that love and emotion is pent up inside him. He's just waiting for the right moment to release the surging tide into the dry, parched earth that awaits life's nutrients. He lingers, wondering, perhaps, if he should sweep me up and lay me on the bed. Just as I enter the realm of expectation, he says, 'Suppose we better get going. Your Tracey's waiting for us.'

And she is. In all the excitement, the first real excitement I've experienced for years, I clean forgot that Tracey is waiting downstairs, probably imagining all sorts of illicit goings-on.

We race down the winding marble staircase. Tracey gawks at me. I flush with embarrassment, although I do manage to emulate my choir girl look of old which hopefully allays Tracey's X-rated impression of our prolonged absence. Perhaps she perceives my glowing aura the result of an activity I've never engaged in.

Normal personas restored, we head into the courtyard overlooking the hotel's swimming pool and sit to our evening meal. Tracey and I do the well-mannered thing and eat very little, while Wayne demonstrates his huge appetite by downing a prawn cocktail and huge steak in the time it takes us to eat a small serve of rice and chicken.

I've no doubt that Tracey feels awkward. Between us we manage to communicate on a variety of topics. Wayne's accent is difficult to understand as I suppose mine is to him. I have no difficulty understanding English when spoken by Americans, but the British English is so different. Most noticeable are the vowels which seem to be clipped and chopped into very short pieces as if there's not enough time to say the whole word. Take, for instance, the word 'downtown'. We sort of sing that word, with an almost southern American drawl. D-o-w-n-t-o-w-n; by the time we have said it, you're almost there! Wayne, on the other hand, says it so fast that you've driven through without even realising.

We canvass the regular first-meeting trivialities: his flight, his work, my home life and the weather. Gee, how he complains about the heat. And this is nearly eight o'clock at night! He's yet to experience the stifling 28 to 35 degrees of the day, a normal day for me and Tracey, but for him it will be like sitting in a Turkish steam bath. I mean, where the heck does he think he is? Hasn't he checked out a map to see that we're just north of the equator?

The next day I introduce Wayne to my family: my father Jackson, and brothers Jacob, Jaden and Jason who join us at the table.

All right. You want to know if I'm exercising that poetic licence stuff with my family names. No way. I'm not writing this as a piece of fiction where the writer simply plucks characters from a baby names book, or invents them with the ease of drawing them out of a hat. Do you really doubt that parents would name their children so? Be assured that I have no motive to lead you astray or denigrate my parents. I don't know how common the practice is, but I think my father might have been a little egotistical, naming all the children with a 'Ja' prefix. The only difference is that we're not *famous* like those Kardashian kids whose names all 'kommence' with 'K' – with the noted exception of Rob. (What we do not know is whether he has changed his name from 'Keith' or 'Kevin'.)

So what did my mama say about that, you might ask? Probably nothing. She would have deferred to papa's wishes: they're the names and that's that! Maybe that's where the rift started with mama and me – she didn't want me named Jacinta – probably wanted a nice catholic name like Mary. Mama's never forgiven him, and has vented her anger by continuing to pretend that I don't exist. I don't know whether papa always got his way, but he certainly got the better end of the stick – and still does – as they say in the American movies.

Wayne sits at one end of the kitchen table, strategically positioned where the cooling draught of our rickety fan blows directly over his face. It makes no difference. Tiny beads of perspiration drip from his forehead to his shirt. Yuk. I suffer for him. I excuse myself and return with a cool flannel. I feel like a trainee nurse as I wipe his brow. Wayne frowns in embarrassment, but I don't think he is as uncomfortable as am I: I must look like a doting mother caring for her sick child.

We eat the unimaginative chicken *adobo* with rice, fish and salad and follow with ice cream for dessert. It is a reasonable introduction to our rather plain Philippine cuisine. We're not up there with the culinary kings of the world who prepare fancy dishes of exotic treats that few can afford. We eat chicken, fish and pork, accompanied by rice and select locally grown vegetables. No fancy curries or spices, just a splash of vinegar or soy. Plain foods, that's us. Plain Pinoys.

We catch a few local television shows before Wayne asks me to take him for an exploratory walk around the neighbourhood. Perhaps he thinks it'll be cooler outside. It's not. We've already traipsed around a shopping centre during the day. I tell him that I'm feeling tired and would prefer to rest.

The previous night I'd slept in Wayne's hotel room. I know what you're thinking, but it was nothing like that. I hate it when people jump to conclusions and immediately think something untoward is going on as soon as a girl says she's spent time alone with a guy. I slept in his room, yes, but we had separate beds. End of story. If you don't believe that, too bad. But what you may not believe is how nice and gentlemanly Wayne was. He made a point of telling me that he respected my religious beliefs and would not allow anything to happen that would compromise my faith or make me feel uneasy. The unfortunate consequence of that was that I *did* then feel uneasy, because I actually *wanted* something to happen. I hadn't a clue what, but seduction was banging on my forehead. Shamefully, the only seduction I know of is what I've seen in the movies and the, um, er, movies I shouldn't have seen at Mae's.

I'd already drafted the script. We'd be watching television and he'd tell me how glad and lucky he is to be with me. He'd whisper: *Jacinta, I'm so glad I'm here. I would never have found beauty like yours without finding you; I would never have filled the void in my heart and the deep pit of emptiness. I would never have touched the softness and sensitivity of someone so prepared to give her all to me.* He'd lean into my shoulder and kiss my neck and look into my eyes as if seeking permission to kiss me. He'd close his eyes, as would I, and our lips would capture each other, like the gently closing jaws of the ferocious Venus Fly trap. My heart would flutter with impatience as I await his invasion. He'd respond, as if answering my orders. With military precision he'd slip his hand under my shirt and brush the soft flesh of my midriff, encircle my belly button, then trek north, climbing each rib like a skeletal ladder. I don't know how many steps, but it'd feel like about 90 – I'd be so suspended in anticipation, yearning for his fingers to creep closer and closer to the previously prohibited boundaries barricaded by my bra. He'd loiter there for a moment, awaiting my counter attack to sweep his hand away. With no execution of counter-intelligence imminent, he'd continue his mission, probe inside my bra and across uncharted flesh. He'd continue, in delicate sweeping circles, over tiny land mines encircling the home-post of my breast. I would detonate and explode into flashes of fire, sparks and heat, before my inner being rumbled with the ground-swell of tremors emanating from the footsteps of troops as they marched ecstatically into unchartered land. He'd plough through my unresisting front and transgress unchallenged into virgin territory. He'd receive carte-blanch permission to conquer his assignment. All the while my pulse rate would hover around dangerous levels while I wait for him to unhook my bra and take my aching breasts in his hands. And I would submit – like a prisoner yielding to her captor.

Gosh, listen to me. Doesn't that show how much time I spend in front of the television? How I must crave that special attention. Sadly, nothing like that happened. We kissed a couple of times, talked for a while – generally a rehash of all the experiences we'd shared through our emails and letters. We talked about England and the Philippines and some of the similarities they share. Both countries are rich in Christianity, though my country is founded on Catholicism, a legacy of rich Spanish control from the early 1900s. The English devote their faith predominantly through the Church of England which can be traced back to the second century. English religion also boasts numerous changes exhorted by early kings' spiritual leanings. Interestingly, from about the sixteenth century, the English church retained much of the medieval Roman Catholicism framework.

Both countries feature a vast network of churches, many of which challenged architectural standards of their time. Whilst the church has been around since the bible ('house-church' Romans 16:5) some notable testimonies to God date back to the twelfth century.

Our political structures are similar, although the republican Philippines elect a president whereas Britain is headed by monarchical succession of the Queen (or King) with an elected prime minister beneath. Both countries stave off history of rorts and mismanagement through the ages. Some would say the Philippines top the list – never will it recover from the Ferdinand Marcos era when several billion US dollars disappeared from the economy.

SEVEN

OUR CULTURES TOO, ARE DIFFERENT, which I find out by accident when Wayne tries to kiss me in a shopping centre. 'We don't do that in public,' I blush. 'Sharing emotions in public is frowned upon. Not that it's forbidden; it just makes a girl look 'easy'.' This attitude will gradually disappear as American and western influence further shapes our society.

I understand Wayne's confusion. Of course it is hypocritical of me to resist in the shopping mall, yet expect it at the airport. The airport, however, is an exception to the rule because of its transient fusion of cultures. Also, a kiss at an airport is one of welcomes or send-offs rather than a heated exchange of love. Wayne smiles his cheeky grin. 'Wait 'til you get to England. Summer time. Couples lying in parks kissing and cuddling on blankets. Girls in bikinis, guys in bathers. It's all part of normal living. No one takes any notice.'

Wait 'til I get to England? He's thought that *far ahead?*

We wake the following morning, surprised and happy

to see each other in the same room. I'd certainly intended to go home, but had succumbed to sleep deprivation. I don't really know what Wayne expected; maybe that I'd just disappear like a cloud of dust in the middle of the night and blow myself home. I study the ticker-tape of his guilt about what my parents might think. That is very nice of him. But my life has been built on trust. I am now of the age where I can do as I please – within reason. I am proud that he is not just like any other guy whose thought processes are kick-started by sex.

I decline breakfast. My decision upsets him. Technically, I'm not supposed to be in the hotel. He'd paid for a single suite. I know that hotel staff everywhere accept the comings and goings of patrons and their guests, but I do not want to paint myself as a clandestine visitor of the night, of which there are many in the Philippines. I slink out of the hotel and leap onto a motorcycle for the ten peso ride home.

After breakfast I trek to Mae's house, which is perched atop a hill, along with another half a dozen small homes within a stone's throw of each other. And when I speak of 'stone's throw' I mean the floppy-armed toss of a young child. Many of our homes abut each other or are separated by only metres. We have a lengthy discussion about Wayne and my happiness, and about Mae's continued search for her own beau. Then she hits me with a bombshell.

'I could have had him, you know.'

'What do you mean? How could you have? You never even knew about him until I told you.'

'Yes, but he'd emailed me an interest at about the same time he emailed you.'

'No way. He wouldn't do that.'

'It's all right, Cin. He was up-front telling me that he was corresponding with someone else and he didn't want to be seen as two-timing or unfaithful or anything like that. He said he might contact me if the person he was emailing did not work out. Of course I had no idea at the time it was you. Think of all the people registered on *Find a Filipina;* hundreds of thousands of them, and then the most amazing coincidence happens. He sends an interest to us both.'

'Yes. But we did write similar things about ourselves and both want similar traits in the person we seek. Also, I wonder if as we both registered at about the same time, we were both fairly close together on the photos pages?'

'Possible I suppose. I never looked. But in a way I'm sorry, Mae, because it is you who introduced me to the 'net, and now I've got the reward.'

'I'm happy for you. I'll find someone, I've got no shortage of interest on my page.'

'You know what Mae. I am really happy, and Wayne's much nicer than I expected, although I suppose I don't really know what I expected because foreigners are so different to our guys.'

Later in the day I take Wayne for a long excursion to an outer province to visit other family members. While there, we look at available properties. We had spoken of buying a small plot of land as an investment – even at this early stage we are considering our future.

We've discussed marriage, and we've looked at rings in Metro, the big department store. And we've talked about Wayne asking formal permission of my papa. You might think this, too, is premature, because it is only the second day of his visit, but it has not come out of the blue. We frequently discussed it in our emails. After all, it was our reason for joining *Find a Filipina.com*. It is inevitable. We want to make our engagement official and launch into wedding arrangements.

And that's exactly what we do.

That night I bring Wayne home for dinner. He's happy talking with papa, getting by with broken-English conversations about the military and one of papa's long-lost military acquaintances who lives in Manchester. I feel sorry for papa after Wayne sarcastically replies that England is home to a population of fifty-two million [2014] and he has not yet met everyone, including papa's friend. [Author's Note: The *United Kingdom* – as opposed to England – 2014 population was sixty-six million]

The crucial moment is destroyed when my brother crashes through the front door. He knows his place so retreats to his room, leaving me with Wayne and papa. Wayne stands, picks up the television remote and presses 'mute'. Mama nonchalantly wipes benches in the kitchen, not particularly watching or listening, but keenly aware of the silence-filled room.

Wayne looks to me. I shoot him a glare: *Go on, this is*

your job. I smile and attract papa's attention before Wayne splutters, 'We have something to tell you. Correction. Something I should ask you.' Papa looks at mama. They share a knowing gleam in their eye, one I've never seen, as if they are actually *expecting* a major announcement. Wayne doesn't do the down on bended knee thing; he merely flushes a neon pink and says, 'Jacinta and I would like to marry. We, er, seek your blessing.'

Papa swings into the role of protective father. Gives Wayne the look-after-my-daughter-or-I'll-come-and-get-you lecture, to which Wayne replies, 'You'll have no need to do that Mr Sequentez.'

I nearly crack up. 'Mr Sequentez,' he called him. I don't think papa has been called that in nearly half a century. 'Call me Jackson,' papa replies as he flips the caps off two San Miguel's to drink to our impending marriage.

We have no idea of the administrative nightmare ahead, and if my experience serves to assist you find your own foreigner, I must be very candid and forewarn you of the many hurdles you'll have to leap over enroute to marriage.

I first have to obtain a 'Certificate of Singleness' issued by the National Statistics Office. This little document satisfies a priest or celebrant that a woman is, in fact, single, and not trying to evade a bad marriage by bigamously marrying another man whether he be a foreigner or Philippine national. The problem with attending the NSO, as most locals know, is that one has to take with them two litres of water and two meals, because we need at least that much sustenance to survive the potential three hour wait in either full sun or pouring rain. In fairness, I should specify that I refer to the Cebu office and that I reflect only on my own experience.

One has to be meticulously prepared to progress through the bureaucratic checks and double-checks. Take as many forms of identification as possible: student cards, bank cards, licences or photo cards, and anything else that *officially* verifies your identity. Stating the obvious, we also need our Birth Certificate.

An appointment must be made with the appropriate church and pre-marriage counselling undertaken by both parties to the marriage. I think it's strange how a couple is required to receive divine instruction and counselling about being married, but if that's the way it is, we must accept it. Wayne tells me that there's no such requirement in England. I reckon that if there were, there wouldn't be so many failed marriages.

During the rapidly dissolving fortnight we experience quite a few, might I say 'cultural' issues that compromise our one hundred percent harmony. In all my eagerness and dreams of love and romanticism, I've never thought about the 'down side' – the moments of indecision, disagreement and differences of opinion *any* two people will encounter during their relationship. I've never needed to know how to avoid conflict and embarrassment. So I now face the prospect of having to learn a whole new behavioural characteristic: submission.

There is a western-world belief that all Asian women are submissive and subservient. I don't know how or from where that originated. I fit well with society. My role is clearly espoused in the bible, which anoints the male as provider and protector. Even by implication, that places the woman's status beneath the male – she will devote time to homemaking and child-rearing. Please don't paint me with the politically incorrect labels I see plastered over American and British television and newspapers. I'm just saying how it is and how my upbringing has contributed to my views. I know the downside (and I've seen the results) of women who are suppressed and dominated by their supposedly 'superior' and 'upstanding' husbands who beat them if the dinner's not ready on time; who throw them against a wall if they've spent ten pesos too much on shopping; and who animalistically rape them after the poor woman refuses his advances because she is too tired or has 'it'.

Yes, we might be submissive to those we love. But no, we aren't an instant cleaner, on-call housemaid, or a 'lift-your-skirt-and-give-it-to-me-when-I-want-it' convenience. Wake up. Times have changed. *I* am strong-willed – a trait I will not relinquish for anyone.

I consider some of the inconsequential matters that embroil us in dissention. Perhaps we are both embarrassed about tiny indifferences precipitating mammoth catastrophes that see me race home to spend the afternoon crying, stretched across my bed. Mama uncharacteristically offers consolation.

I fob her off, almost rudely: 'Nothing mum. We'll never get on. He doesn't understand me.'

'Give it time,' she says. 'He is different; you will have differences just as papa and I have, although we much keep to our own now.'

I know mama is right. I haven't given our budding relationship a chance.

I do the same at school. I fix on something and then pursue it until I've proven to anyone and everyone that I am right. I take a stance like a political opposition member and pursue my cause, even when I know I'm wrong – I just have to push the point until I win. That is all well and good, until you try that strategy with someone like Wayne, because he is exactly the same. In the end we both fight, verbally, not physically. He wins because of his better English comprehension. I really wish we could debate in Cebuano so that I could hold the advantage for once.

Yeah, he is 'different'. I gradually find out just how different he is. He is different in the way he treats me with such love and care for my well-being. On two days of illness, when I had 'it', he was what one calls a pillar of strength. He made meals, swept the floor and left me to recuperate on the couch. Mama was astounded. I could not have done anything had I tried, but having a companion like Wayne was far better than one who insists on dinner on the table at a certain time, clothes ironed, and having home and garden maintained in such a pristine condition that it would qualify for a feature cover of *Home Beautiful*. Unfortunately, there *are* foreigners with such ideals, like those who seek permanent live-in maids with on-the-side benefits. Beware of that person, because they'll surface when you least expect it. They may offer wealth and clothes galore, but you forego the autonomy of choice to do as you please, when you want, because you are forever at the beck and call of your 'master.'

The other difference in Wayne is that there is something missing. A little piece of life that is locked away in the jewellery box of his mind. Permanently locked. The key thrown away. I often wonder if I've said something wrong to cause a small fragment of his life to rise and release itself in a diffused temper tantrum. This doesn't happen very often, but when it does, it disarms me; it makes me wonder what really is behind the facade. In the big picture, it causes no damage so I learn to accept that as part of his character.

Perhaps we all have a compartment of classified life material we withhold from loved ones. I certainly have mine. Preservation of soul and prevention of potential embarrassment becomes paramount because we seek to insulate even those closest to us from the horrors of childhood, the terrors of our teenage years, or transgressions of our early adult life. Even those of us with devout religious conviction cannot see ourselves confessing these historical aberrations of our soul, so they remain, like centuries' old stains on cathedrals – seen but unable to be removed except by scrubbing hard the very fabric of their construction.

In the final analysis, it doesn't worry me. I live for

now and Wayne is mine. He's made a significant change to my life, for the better, and I have a great future to look forward to. We are planning our wedding, and I am set to move overseas and start a new life. Everything has progressed at such a rate; it is as if I am caught in a whirl-wind – and I want to stay in it. Wayne is eager for me to move to England as soon as possible to marry. That is another minor conflict because I want my special day at home, in the company of my large extended family and friends. I cave in, believing that to start on the right foot I should appease Wayne as best I can. We start the visa application.

EIGHT

IT ACTUALLY HAPPENS SOME MONTHS later. There's not much to tell about the interim. We continue to email and write; maintain our weekly Skype and chat sessions and exchange documents pertaining to sponsorship, financial declarations and other immigration-related requirements.

The preparatory paperwork flows much easier than I expected. Once lodged, it takes only a matter of weeks before I am asked to attend a Bureau of Immigration interview in Manila, to verify that the relationship and impending marriage is genuine. That presents no problems to us because I've kept all of Wayne's letters and photos since we got together. As I've said, some seek to leave our country under false pretences solely for the purpose of commencing a better life. There are also those who enter marriages to escape the Philippines, only to divorce a few years later after citizenship of their new country has been granted.

Wayne transfers the appropriate airfare plus some spending money and encourages me to also use the trip to visit another of my aunties who lives in Manila. Amazingly, there is no interview facility available in Cebu (the second largest city in the Philippines).

The interview results arrive in early December, enabling us to plan my flight to England. I clutch my Fiancée Visa which allows me to remain in England under the condition that I marry my sponsor (Wayne) within six months. I am so happy – I would marry him tomorrow.

Around this time I learn that Mae is corresponding with a guy in America, some cold part the name of which I do not remember. She is happy for me, and I am equally happy for her. In one way I am a little disappointed that I, too, am not going to America. I know little about England, partly because I haven't spent any time learning about my new country. My whole focus is directed to Wayne and my future.

With family gathered by my side at the airport, the reality of my upheaval materialises. I know not when I will see my family: mother, father, brothers, aunties, uncles, nephews and nieces, and all the school and work friends I hold close to my heart. Simple chores like walking to the store or the mall, once so routine, now become incidental to my life. I won't do that again in Cebu. I fear I will even lose my language, because from this day forward, English will be my only means of communication.

The hugs and kisses and tears of farewells accompany me during the flight like refugees stowing away in my head. I try to evict them by thinking of Wayne and the future – to no avail. I am supposed to be bubbling with joy and expectation. Instead, fear and sorrow take over. For a girl who thinks marrying a foreigner will be one huge adventure, let the following bring you back to earth.

In the emotional environment of the departure lounge it is easy to accept hugs and farewells. We're all smiles. Tears are camouflaged or wiped into beloveds' shoulders; we're receiving chocolates and cards and magazines and teddies; and we're arranging phone calls and texts and letters. We experience the ultra-high of the last hugs and kisses; and we wave farewell, knowing that we are a plane flight from the start of an exciting new life.

Only after take-off do we accept that there's no going back – at least not in the short term. We're on a journey to the unknown. The love we have fostered over previous months or years might count for nothing. We are now a chattel – an item to be owned by another person. We can't simply withdraw and catch a bus or taxi back to our parents' or a relative's home. We'll be isolated. Imprisoned in our new country.

There can be no doubt that our fiancé wants the best for us, but he will not know or understand our inner turmoil. We feel a huge loss because family is the backbone of our existence. Once that is removed or inaccessible, we crumple to the floor. It matters not what joys and expectations lie before us. We've left behind our history, culture and belonging. We slump to the depths of depression. Admission to adulthood creates its own destiny. We don't consider that we *can* pick up where we left off, which, of course, we *could* do by booking a return flight – but only if we have the funds, or if our fiancé will pay it. That is an alarming proposition.

So I am like a clown juggling feelings when I wheel my two bags into Heathrow Airport's arrival's hall. The sight of Wayne lifts my spirits. The future has just trounced the past.

I have to admit that I'm initially disappointed with England. The first thing I notice after leaving the airport is that all the trees appear dead. I ask Wayne about them. For a moment he looks puzzled before telling me that some English trees are 'deciduous', which means that they shed their leaves each winter as the tree becomes dormant. Not dead, he explains, just in a hibernated state so they can preserve themselves against winter's cold.

And it is cold. So cold. Colder than I ever imagined cold could be. I feel as if I am trapped in a supermarket fridge. I'll spend the winter shivering, trying to adapt to temperatures as low as minus two degrees. I'll have to set the home heating to the max. Yes, I'll miss Cebu.

After sitting in a plane for half a day and a whole night, I have to endure a further three and a half hour journey in Wayne's car to the strangely named town of Torquay. (Maybe it's strange because I had no idea how to pronounce it). On entering his flat I am confronted by balloons and decorations. Over the door hangs a huge welcome banner with snippets of our history and conversations scrawled in felt pen surrounding the words 'Welcome Jac.' On seeing my name spelt as 'Jac', I consider ripping down the sign, but then excuse him because of the effort he'd put in to make me feel at home. I put it down to his warped sarcasm.

The first thing we do, well, let's make that the second, is to scurry to the local shops to outfit me in suitable clothes. We purchase warm fluffy pyjamas, jumpers, track suits and a coat, fluffy slippers, gloves and scarf. I walk out of the shop looking more English than some of the English, save for my indifferent complexion.

We drop into a café where I learn that I'm in for a major diet change. Everything is so 'foreign'. Sure, they have McDonald's – but no Jollibee. There are Indian curries and papadams, French croissants and baguettes, Greek Kebabs and Giros. The English have their Cornish Pasties, Fish and Chips, and pub meals. Some of the pub meals offer extraordinary value. They would constitute a banquet back home. (Sorry, I'll always call Cebu 'home'). I have an Assorted Basket that contains a piece of fish, scallops, prawns, 14 chicken wings and a giant serving of chips. Wayne devours a humongous burger with melting cheese and strips of bacon hanging out of buns which struggle to contain two huge beef patties. He also accepts a huge serve of chips which he scoffs with 10 of *my* chicken wings. We wash it down with a 'pint' (568 ml) of Pepsi Max. We will never have a problem with leftover food.

Within days, we attend the registry office to book our wedding. We learn of a stumbling block that requires our residing in the county (like a *barangay*) for six weeks prior to the marriage. That is okay for Wayne; he's been here for ages, but for me it means we have to change our plans. It isn't a major inconvenience. The registrar finds a timeslot a few weeks hence, which turns out to be Saturday, February fourteen. Valentine's Day. The very day Wayne and I first 'officially' met in Cebu. That suits my sentimental nature just fine.

A welcome benefit is that once married, I can apply for permanent residency, provided I remain married to Wayne. That won't be a problem. I don't ever want to leave his side. And then, following a two year probationary period, I can apply for British citizenship. Two years seems so far away.

Wedding preparations bring further disappointment, though I'm careful to not reveal my pain. I expected a flamboyant procession heading to a historic church, bridesmaids and flower girls trailing behind, photographers snapping cheery passers-by, and a video camera recording every smile, hug and kiss. We will have none of that. Wayne has been divorced only a short time, leaving him with very little cash reserves. At first, I selfishly forget to take into account the money he spent on visa and immigration fees, airfares both to Manila and to England, and the small weekly amounts he unfailingly sent me.

I buy a dress and shoes off eBay and Wayne hires a suit from a local outfitter. He scores a posy of flowers from a street vendor and wraps it in baking foil from our kitchen. Sure, it's the thought that counts, but that is so far removed from my original thoughts of a spectacular bouquet of assorted wildflowers and orchids, all wrapped in crinkly red cellophane. That's not all I miss out on.

I waive trying on dresses and shoes with Mae and the bridesmaids; assigning the girls projects to arrange everything from venues to bridal cars; and I forego losing myself to cocktails on the infamous hen's night.

February fourteen is bitterly cold. And stays that way. I am expected to walk the aisle in a dress cut low across the bodice, exposing my chest, shoulders and upper back to the near freezing elements. I bake myself in the car for a few moments before snuggling into Wayne for the brisk walk into the registry office.

The guests list isn't exactly exhaustive. It comprises two guys from Wayne's part-time evening job. There should have been three, but one cancelled at the last moment. Fortunately, two is the minimum amount of witnesses required for an English wedding. I would hate to scour the streets, pleading for a couple of strangers to witness what should be the happiest day of my life. But you know what? I am happy. No matter the compromises and circumstances; I am about to be married. The fairy tale dreams now stand for nothing. This is the real deal and things will surely improve from here.

Won't they?

So what is a girl supposed to feel on her wedding day? Joy? Elation? A life-changing experience that defines the future life to be shared between the new couple? From a very young age girls across the world imagine themselves as fairies and princesses. Some parents even call their daughters princess. As we grow up, we marvel at weddings, at the beautiful, billowing white taffeta, lace and satin dresses with flowing trains held by pretty maids; we share the happiness and beaming smiles of parents, friends and the bride and groom; and then we spend years in anticipation of replicating those very experiences we actually *felt* in our heart – just waiting for the right guy and the right day.

For me it is a bit of a letdown. I listen to a few words in an old school building, say 'I do' a couple of times, and listen to a woman admit that the powers vested in her allow her to pronounce us man and wife. That is it. Man and wife. A new entity. No longer Jacinta Sequentez. I've lost my identity and my heritage. I am now Jacinta S. Dunlop, having followed our custom of retaining our former family name as a middle initial.

I consider embracing the British tradition of creating names by retaining my maiden name and dropping in a hyphen. Jacinta Sequentez-Dunlop. Now there's a name. I feel for my future children should they be burdened with a multi-syllable name like Felicity or Margaret. What a mouthful: Felicity Sequentez-Dunlop. No, I wouldn't do that to a child, so I settle for the plain old Dunlop. Little do I know that I will later be known as Jac Tyre – for obvious reasons. Yeah, the laughs will all be on me: 'Why don't you *roll* around for a few drinks?' 'How about a few *rubbers* of tennis?' 'Has *inflation* affected your savings?' 'Do you *tread* water when you go swimming?' 'Have you ever had it off with the *Michelin* man?' But the one that'll really get me is when I participate in some sort of debate and my opponent says, 'Oh, Jac Tyre, just like your name, you're so full of hot air.' So yeah, I'll hear them all – the little niggles that seem so second-nature to the English. They'll all think they are comedians, but the end result will be that people's feelings are at stake and no one ever seems to give a damn.

After the wedding, our photographer, a budget retiree sourced from the local paper, takes a few snaps around the registry office, and then reneges on an agreement to take more shots in the beautiful surrounds of the River Avon. He claims he is double booked, but more than likely he just wants to return to the warmth of his home to watch football. Warning: beware of budget anything. The English have a saying: 'You only get what you pay for.'

The guests depart after the ceremony. I am ashamed because I thought Wayne would have at least encouraged them to accompany us to the pub for a meal and a few drinks. Only then do I realise that his finances are so well and truly shot. So we go home, change, and head straight back to a local Thai restaurant where we have our wedding breakfast – our first *official* meal as a married couple.

I feel reserved, despondent. An inexplicable emotional wave devours me. I slump from the wedding ceremony's half-hour high, which is really no more than an artificial environment driven by dreams and adrenalin. When I returned to reality I fell flat on my face. Don't ask how I know this, but the feeling replicates coming off a heroin high – we've enjoyed the twinkling stars and rainbows; we're now scraping parched earth with our fingernails desperate to find a tiny grain to provide the next hit.

NINE

So THE NEW MRS JACINTA S. Dunlop is now house-bound and fully dependant on her foreigner.

Wayne, in trying to recover from the debilitating effects of a financial clean-out from his divorce, sidelined his handyman work in favour of a guaranteed regular income. I feel guilty because it is for me that he sacrificed work he enjoys, solely to ensure our security and future. He's taken on two jobs. Between 8.30 and 5.00 p.m. he struggles through repetitious tasks in a factory. From there he drives twelve miles to a part-time evening job to load delivery trucks from 6.00 p.m. to 11.00 p.m. That becomes a 5 days-per-week routine.

He arrives home at 11.20. I wait up for him with a hot meal steaming on the table. He gulps it down, tries to do the right thing by chatting with me for a few minutes – in front of the television – and then trips off to bed. And sleeps. Straight away. I know he is tired, but I am upset that he seems to not want to make time for me. But that's not the end of it. Come Saturday morning he's off to work overtime from 6.00 a.m. until midday.

I am devastated. I'd expected nothing like this. I am abandoned; left on my own to flick through magazines and television shows that do nothing to nurture the harmony and companionship I crave. I revisit my former hobby of window shopping. After peering into the same dozen windows every day, my enthusiasm evaporates. I walk just to get out of the home.

'Make some friends,' Wayne suggests.

Get real, I feel like saying. Do I just walk up to a stranger in the street and ask: 'Would you like to be my friend?' It's easy for him, around people all day, always actively engaged.

There were times in the Philippines when I felt exactly the same: the final days of school holidays after friendships had frayed through overexposure and parents were jack of us moping about the house because we'd spent our small allowance, leaving us with nothing to do and nowhere to go. In desperation, we'd walk aimlessly around the streets, head downcast, not seeing anyone or anything. History repeats. *I've come all this way for this?*

I know he cares for me, but doesn't recognise, or accept, my situation. One day he tells me about a Filipina in a local shop and suggests I go to see her, to acquaint ourselves and perhaps exchange some of our own interests. I need that. By the time I pluck the courage to visit, I haven't spoken my own language for six weeks.

The meeting spawns a whole new circle of friends, two of whom are Lena and Mal. Lena has lived in England for twenty years after leaving Cebu to marry her foreigner. Our similar backgrounds lead to a strong friendship. Lena locks me in her heart. Before long, I'm addressing her as mama Lena – our customary form of respect.

Wayne sees glimpses of my former self so insists I phone home at least once a week to maintain family relationships. He even offers to help get me a job, despite a visa condition restricting me from working for the first six months of residency. But there is a 'grey area' and Wayne is one for exploiting grey areas. The visa is ambiguous about whether or not I can work during the whole term of the Fiancée Visa, or only while I am unmarried. He applies a loose construction to the grammatical interpretation and deems that I am allowed to work because I am now married. He does not confirm his reasoning with the Bureau of Immigration – just in case he is wrong.

Wayne types up a résumé and accompanies me to the personnel agency which had helped him enter the workforce. Within days I have a job in the same factory as Wayne, although we are tasked to different departments. Now absorbed with an interest – even though the work is mundane – I have independence and my own income. I am feeling better and *nearly* happy.

I have not worked since my weekend factory job in the Philippines nearly twelve months' earlier. The different, or relaxed, work ethics shock me. Back home we were not allowed to talk on the production line. Here, women talk and joke, mostly about husbands and sex, and they play around and take long toilet breaks to sneak cigarettes and re-apply make-up. Back in my factory, we had to ask a supervisor's permission to attend the toilet – even if we were busting.

On returning home, I resume the five evenings per week solitary confinement. Wayne finally recognises my heartache and starts taking sick days to keep me company. That propels him to worry about his reliability and work ethic. Ultimately, he decides that rather than suffer a possible bad reference, he'll resign. I am more than a little embarrassed that he has sacrificed his job for me, but I am happy that at last we can spend quality time together. We enjoy Friday night dinners at restaurants and evenings out with new friends. A proper marriage begins to assemble itself.

I enjoy travelling to and from work, sharing the early morning with Wayne; seeing my first snow drifts across undulating British terrain, talking about things that we never seemed to have time to talk about at home, and planning our future. Oh, how I want a child. I have done so since I was a young girl. I don't really know why, other than to think that I've been blessed with an overabundance of maternal instinct. Wayne already has three children of his own. I haven't met them, but I've seen photos. He had a vasectomy after the birth of his last child three years' earlier. Friends have told me that vasectomies are irreversible. Wayne insists otherwise. That's one of the problems with the friends' network; neither reliable nor accurate. Also from the friends' network I heard stories of wedding night catastrophes. I'm hardly going to reveal all that happens in our bedroom, but yes, the first night was, well… scary. Of course I knew what to expect, and in a way I looked forward to it, but nervousness overtook excitement. The whole thing was awful; I singed with pain and wondered if it would ever be the pleasurable experience others have described. Suffice to say that I am more at ease with it now.

For the next few months I fret at the onset of my period. I wonder if I will ever get pregnant. I attach credibility to my friend's opinion about vasectomy reversals. In desperation, or more realistically, concern, we attend my doctor where I suffer an embarrassing examination. (Perhaps it's only embarrassing because I didn't know what to expect). I am relieved to find that there is nothing wrong with me.

'There's nothing wrong with me.' Sorry, I guess that really is a bad turn of phrase. As women, we think we'll conceive instantly – that we'll get pregnant from an impromptu five-minute quickie or one-night-stand. Whilst in some cases that does happen, (and usually to those least expecting it) in general we are too impatient to allow nature to take its course to reward us with pregnancy on its own terms. But nature is unkind to *us*, and even Wayne wonders if he might be the problem, despite a post-vasectomy reversal test proving that he is capable of fathering a child, or many. He too sees a doctor.

Months roll on and still the magic evades us. We resort to booking IVF assistance, but amazingly, only one week out from our appointment, I find that I am pregnant. That is another memorable moment I've stored away. After waiting so many years I am now fulfilled. Not one bit concerned that it is 3.00 a.m. in the Philippines, I phone mama and tell her the news.

A huge shift occurs after finding that I'm pregnant. My dreams and prayers have been answered – not that I've been doing much praying of late. Sure, Wayne has accompanied me to church a few times, but I feel that he tags along as a sense of duty, rather than following religious convictions – if he really has any. Nevertheless, I am happy and about to start re-mapping my life as both a wife and mother.

I've said I have long yearned for a child; the earliest pangs surfaced when I was just fourteen. I will say that there had been many opportunities back home. A girl can have a child as easy as catching a cold from a summer downpour. There's never a shortage of willing partners to help our cause. I am not of that type. I have waited and married so that my child will grow up in a home shared by loving and responsible parents.

My lifestyle changes little in the early stages of pregnancy, aside from my body's adjustment to the formation of a new life: the morning sickness; the sore back;

the revised diet and drinking habits; and the wavering interest of libidinal yearnings.

Sometimes joy is temporary, destined to be only short-lived, perhaps as a test. Whether as a test of character and resilience or a test of our faith in God, I do not, and will not, ever know. My joy and elation is dramatically cut short when I attend the hospital for a regulation twelve-week scan. Wayne dutifully and lovingly accompanies me. I expose my tiny bump to a nurse who smears messy gel over the small rise and presses a cold ultra-sound wand across my warm flesh. I try to decipher her concerned look. She searches and probes and finally utters: 'Excuse me.' She leaves the room.

Moments later she's back with a doctor. He repeats the scanning process, up and down, left to right. I begin to wonder if he's using my tummy as a Ouija board. He sits me up, places the stethoscope on my back, has a muted conversation with the nurse, and then leaves the room.

The nurse wipes my tummy and sits down. Looks at me and glances to Wayne. 'Sorry. There's no heartbeat.'

I am devastated. I wonder why I'm the chosen one to experience the catastrophe. I have been so careful with my diet. I don't smoke, (and never have) I don't drink and I eat very healthily, aside from a few desserts and chocolate – which I eat solely for the calcium content. Wayne too, is upset. He is more upset for me than he is for himself. That might be just a male thing. I don't know for sure. He's proven that even during our fiercest moments he has the greatest respect and concern for my welfare.

The nurse continues: 'Sometimes these things happen. There's no reason or cause for it; it just wasn't meant to be.'

I hate it when people offer those patronising comforters. Surely there's a reason. I don't understand all the medical terminologies, but I have learnt that about 10 to 25 percent of known pregnancies are lost due to miscarriage in the first six weeks of pregnancy, due primarily, to the close proximity of the forthcoming period at which time the embryo / foetus is 'flushed' out.

I don't know what to do for the remainder of the day other than cry away the afternoon in bed.

Look at the picture. Here's a girl who has pursued her dreams and is well on the way to achieving them. She has recently married, secured a good job and has a nice home. Life is great. She's started the 'baby collection': nappies, body suits, bathing necessities. She's accumulated catalogues for prams and cots and car seats and she has the dreams of her son or daughter crawling around in her home. One can't throw all that aside.

I phone Mae, bawl my eyes out and feel immediate relief from her mature words of consolation: 'See it as a new beginning, Cin.'

Move on, I tell myself. I have no option other than to do just that. Time heals all wounds – or so it is said.

Setting the tragedy aside, our lifestyle and compatibility continue to improve despite the niggling arguments and disagreements that form a corridor of darkness through our marriage. Perhaps we married before knowing enough about each other. I have a philosophy about that and it revolves around our being first acquainted on the internet. I think the internet's function is both good and bad in nurturing relationships. On the positive side, both parties have an ideal opportunity to get to know each other without the pressures of physical attraction dominating their senses.

Wayne and I had not exchanged photos during our early weeks of corresponding. I think it might have been about six weeks before we did so. That was due more to my unfamiliarity of transferring photos from phone to computer. The internet café I used did not have modern or 'high tech' equipment. It was difficult to upload photos; they had to be scanned in from a hard copy. A reliable connection was needed, and, because of the file size – even for a small photo – the actual upload was time lost in the café. Now, of course, file sizes are compressed and internet speeds are so much faster. A photo can be loaded in a matter of seconds and one can simply upload from a phone or USB memory stick. Anyway, we wrote our own histories, Wayne more so than me because of my limited English; well maybe not so much limited, it was just harder to find the right words in a language I rarely use. Besides, Mae had drafted out only the bare essentials. 'Never give too much away,' she said. 'You must present an air of mystery.'

Over time we learnt a lot about each other. I treasured Wayne's glossy portraits, just as he was delighted with mine. We often joked about what we would have done had we not liked what we saw. Maybe we cloud the truth in our response. I say, 'I'd love you just the same.' Wayne evades the question: 'It's speculation. We never got to that situation so I don't know what I would have done.'

That's negative enough to make me worry. Thankfully, the situation never presented itself.

TEN

SOME MONTHS LATER, WAYNE CHANGES jobs to another factory which he claims to be the best and cleanest factory in Britain. The factory's product is laminated credit cards, phone cards and secure entry cards. He works a rotating day and afternoon shift which again upsets me because I am left alone in the evenings. The trade-off is his higher income which enables us to buy a few more things for our flat.

One afternoon Wayne tells me of vacancies in the factory and asks if I would be interested. Of course I am because I had to leave my previous job because of transport difficulties. I attend the interview and all goes well until they ask for references. I have my folder of certificates and references from the Philippines, but the interviewer wants a verbal reference, such is the high level of security clearance required for staff. I supply the manager's name of my former factory job. A few weeks later I start work (again) with my husband, initially in the same area, but later in a separate department.

We are in one of those jobs where everything goes great until we're infected by the 'over-exposure' disease. Perhaps our working together, having meal breaks together, and living together fosters abrasion. I tend to think he incites conflict. But in the throes of matrimonial spats, who can define exactly how smooth silk weaves into coarse denim? Who cares? What we should care about is resolving our problems before it's too late.

Regrettably, we did not face our problems until it *was* too late. We disagreed about the smallest things like the price of a home-delivered pizza, and then we didn't talk to each other for days. I considered myself master of 'the silent treatment' – until I discovered that Wayne had duxed the class.

Our evenings become intolerable. Would anyone possibly believe that one of us simply rises from the lounge room couch and casually walks off to bed without even a word? No kiss. No goodnight. Just an ignorant, ill-mannered departure like a train pulling out of a station without a final platform announcement. Then later on, the other one of us climbs into bed, in silence, wondering if our beloved partner is asleep or simply pretending to be so. The next morning we rise, independently get ready for work, make our own individual breakfast, and then – displaying the greatest insult ever to a partner – drive the fifteen mile, 30-minute trip to work in total silence. We purposely avoid each other at work, stagger our meal breaks to ensure there is no possible chance of crossing paths, and then duplicate the process in the evening. Welcome to married life.

After sharing the pain of lost days from our lives, we make a pact to never go to bed without saying goodnight to each other. We successfully work through that period, rendering life much more enjoyable and more to my expectations of what a marriage should be. We earn a good income, and overtime rewards us with funds enough to finance a two week holiday in the Philippines.

Around this time, Wayne is struggling with stalled ambition. He is not entirely happy with factory work. He is a man of high ideals, but seems unable to make money with his mind as would a switched-on salesman, stock-broker or entrepreneur. He is more of a 'hand's on' technician. I guess he would crucify me for my interpretation, because he would counter with the statement that it is his 'mind' that conceived his Home Handyman business which in turn returned him a good income. However, I reckon when it comes to comparing incomes, a tradesperson will earn nowhere near the hourly remuneration of a professional salesperson.

Wayne mentioned his work when we first met online. He must have earned good money to manage the few trips to Cebu before I finally flew to England. We had discussed starting a business in Philippines. I spelt out the difficulties my own people suffer through trying to earn enough to survive. Wayne expected to earn the same (relatively speaking) as he had back home. Not a chance; that would not happen. For a start, there is very little domestic work in Philippines, save for the executive and government estates that are rich in money. Most of those home owners however, employ (or exploit) maids and gardeners for only a few pesos per hour.

The biggest setback is that Filipinos wouldn't consider him. They'd contract their fellow countrymen, at the same time wondering why the heck a 'foreigner' was trying to carve out a labouring career in the Philippines. I suggested the only business in which foreigners succeed is alcohol – bars and clubs. 'Site one of those in the right place,' I said, 'and you're set for life. You'll see more money than you'll ever make as a handyman.' I added that competitive building leases combined with low wages and overheads meant that such a business would surely be a success – 'provided you slip a wad of money under the table for 'special protection'.'

Wayne confided that he was not really a 'people person' and would never be happy in that sort of environment. That was one of the rare occasions he bowed to my advice.

Our holiday 'back home' is memorable, though uneventful – if a vacation can be described in such a manner. We do the usual tourist things: spend time with family, shop, lounge around picture theatres and the beach, and enjoy family outings. When we return, I feel as if we've done nothing in the two weeks away that I could not have done had we remained in England.

Wayne regurgitates his business idea and embarks on redeveloping stationery and researching prices of various supplies, advertising and taxation requirements. One day he simply announces: 'I think I'll get my business going again.' From there it just snowballs. Again I am left alone while he toys with paperwork. I seek solace from the television, night after night.

I welcome the weekends. We rise early, or at least he does. I prefer my sleep-in, to regain the week's lost hours and to restore the energy levels I'll so desperately need for Saturday and Sunday shopping, socialising and, er, romance. As I've said, there's no way I'm going to open up my intimate life, but just let me say that Wayne is so desperately tired during the week. As soon as he arrives home from work, even if I am home at the same time, he's more interested in cat-napping for a couple of hours than sharing shenanigans with me. Maybe that's why I have difficulties getting pregnant! So it could be neglect, loneliness and desire that sends me trawling through social networking and dating sites. Again.

Sure, I have my foreigner; my loving husband and a great life paved before me. But some of the many roads that glisten with wealth and riches crumble at the edges, sometimes due to poor construction, other times due to poor maintenance. I know our preparation was slight – but thorough; our maintenance, on the other hand, is in neglect. We have a marriage decaying from the inside, like a rotting peach – all pure and fuzzy on the surface, but look deeper and there's nothing holding the flesh together.

I wonder how easy it would be to deceive Wayne. I

don't have the deliberate intent to deceive; it's more the thought of what I might be able to get away with. I'm sure I'll have no problem at all. I love Wayne with all my heart, but I also love life – and I am starved of life. I join a couple of websites, upload photos from my album and rework my redundant profile. I change little of the content, even leaving the section where I advise my status as, 'single, seeking a friend, pen-pal or marriage prospect.'

My email box swells with attention. I guiltily share my life with strangers I never should entertain. I update Mae with news, traumas, sadness, highs, lows and just about every other facet of my faux-marriage and new home.

Mae replies with news of my close cousin, Della, whose name is actually Delores – a name I recall she abandoned in her first year of school. Della also commenced a similar journey to mine, with the difference that she married an American rather than an Englishman. She made her home in one of the sunny states of USA while I shiver in two to three degree temperatures, slide on frozen footpaths, try to insulate my fingers in sheepskin mittens – all while relishing the poetic pleasure of standing under winter's first snowfall.

We share a lot in common, having left our home and family to start a new life with a foreigner. We also share many misgivings of the mixed culture marriage, the interpretation (or misinterpretation) of language being just one. Despite having learnt English at school, we are far from fluent. We always revert to our domestic tongue when speaking with fellow Filipinos. I sometimes wish our husbands would place more emphasis on learning Cebuano or Tagalog. Perhaps then, they would comprehend the difficulties *we* face.

By coincidence, Della bore a child soon after marriage and that, I'm proud to say, helps me believe that I too will one day meet my success. Della goes on to confide in me problems within her own marriage and *her* succumbing to online friendships in chat rooms. At first I am astounded that she'd do something like that, but it doesn't take long for me to reflect and realise that her needs for comfort and security are no different than mine. We have both been transplanted in a new country and are simmering with excitement and desire but have no husband or immediate accessible family with whom to share our life.

I am even more astounded – shocked even – when Della tells me that she's arranged a weekend rendezvous with her chat room beau at an undisclosed hotel. She doesn't name the hotel, not for fear of my trust, but more of fear of her message being intercepted by someone, or even worse, her husband.

There is something about women's intuition – an internal sensor, maybe – that warns us when our husbands or partners are unfaithful. You've seen the movies; the errant smudge of lip stick, a train ticket that falls out of the suit pocket – and you finally work out it's a train ticket to nowhere that you've been and nowhere your husband's told you about. The few nights here and there when he phoned and excused himself because an urgent meeting or complication 'has just come up' finally fall into place. Yes, women's intuition. The genetic warning device implanted in our hearts for the express purpose of protecting us from infidelity. I do not know how or why Wayne came to be blessed with this uniquely female phenomenon. Perhaps he'd received a bonus supply of XX chromosomes.

Let me explain: He eases into bed late one evening, cuddles into me and says, 'Hey Cin, nice photo.'

Of course I have no idea what he is talking about. Still half asleep, I mumble, 'What photo?'

'You know. On *Romantic Blossoms* web site.'

I can't reply. I am stunned. I am so stunned I freeze in fear of not knowing what to do or how to handle my dilemma. Perhaps my change in attitude and demeanour had prompted Wayne to look at my internet history. He embarked on a search and find mission and struck gold.

He breaks the ice: 'I took that one didn't I? At the aquarium? Nice touch. Oh, and you're single again? I never got to see the paperwork. Oh well, I'm sure you'll get plenty of replies, but I hope no one at work sees it – it could be so embarrassing for you.'

Despite Wayne's sarcasm and cynicism, the realisation hits me like a punch in the head. (Yes, my brother once did that to me). I've been sprung. I've done nothing wrong, well, not of a great magnitude – I mean I haven't slept with anyone. Of course when I tell Wayne that, it seems to not matter. He says I would have if I could have. I have no idea what I would have done. I don't even know if I would have had enough courage to actually meet anyone face-to-face. I am lonely, vulnerable and so far removed from my comfort zone of family life in the Philippines. That's all it is. A cry for love, companionship and compassion that I can't get at home. I can't explain all that to him; I don't have the English words. And I don't want to show a weakness.

We shout and argue for an hour. I'm surprised neighbours haven't called the police. When we're too tired to continue, we retire to separate rooms.

In the morning, we talk over the situation and the events creating it. Perhaps 'talk' is somewhat of an understatement. There is more arguing and shouting, but no violence thank goodness. Wayne is not like that, but he does finally accept that even though he provides the material foundations of our marriage, he contributes very little to our emotional growth, or more correctly, mine. Strange as it may seem, I cannot understand why he is so oblivious to our situation. I guess it's one of those 'male things' I'll never understand. He tries to convey his absence as being 'for us' – to provide a lifestyle that we'll both enjoy.

I've grown up with next to nothing. Even though I sought material wealth during my quest to find a foreigner, I've also found love, and it is love that supplants my former misguided direction of life.

Wayne spits venom. He professes that our marriage bond is broken; that I have no interest in him because of my venturing behind his back, and because he believes I would have breached my pledge of fidelity – both to him and to God. I can only repeat what I previously said: I do not know what I would have done.

Wayne continues to rant. He suggests I go with whoever I was corresponding because I'd obviously be 'happier', and he suggests I return to the Philippines. Everything he says makes sense because I have both embarrassed him and undermined the exclusive bond of our relationship. I'm sure it is only boredom and excitement that is lacking in my 'part-time' marriage. Had he worked as a 'normal' person in a normal job, I am sure I would have received the love and attention most brides relish and deserve.

How wise we are with the hindsight of reflection. I should never have acted as I did. The regrettable episode forges a landmark in our life. To his credit, we work it through. I offer no rational reason for my behaviour. Perhaps I want to ensure it remains secreted in the depths of my mind. After his tantrum, which at the time I felt was an over-reaction, he is fine.

Yes, we patch our differences over the incident; I think Wayne finally looked deeper into my situation and realised that I could not simply adjust to the new country overnight. Now, I have new friends, a number of them Filipinos who reside in the area, and others I've met through work. I have shoulders to lean on and cry on and hearts to appeal to when I fall deep into the well of depression – as I often do – but not so much of late.

But that will change as my life enters yet another challenging phase.

ELEVEN

WAYNE HAS GROWN IMPATIENT WITH mundane factory life, demonstrated by his sullen demeanour of discontent and underachievement.

In contrast, I want for nothing. Well, maybe not. A girl always wants more. I want life's rewards, but not necessarily material things like flowers, diamonds, dinners and weekends away. I just want to be loved and appreciated. I guess that's where I am short-changed, although I do concede that when Wayne is home – and relaxed – he can be quite romantic. But that is not often enough.

He has not progressed as quickly as he had hoped at work. As a result his impatience festers. I sense he is up to something; I've seen business names and tool companies flick by on internet search screens. I query him, but he brushes it off as, 'Just a bit of research for my old trade.'

He is definitely showing itchy feet to re-establish it. We spend an evening discussing it. I don't mention my hesitation about having only my wage to support us.

Wayne consoles me with his confidence. That's one thing he definitely doesn't lack. Confidence.

The defining moment arrives when night-shift vacancies are advertised on our factory notice board. Coincidentally, one of the positions is one in which Wayne is qualified. 'This is our opportunity,' he tells me thirty seconds after reading it.

'What do you mean?' I ask.

'I can transfer to night-shift, then during the day I can concentrate on getting my business up and running.'

'So when do you sleep?'

'I'm invincible. I don't need much. I've done this before. For much of my life I've worked two jobs.'

Sure enough, Wayne applies for, and is successful in obtaining the night-shift position from 10.00 p.m. to 6.00 a.m. I'm not happy, because I don't really want him gone all night. I don't fare well on my own. I make the sacrifice, again for the sake of our marriage. It presents many difficulties because I continue my rotating day and afternoon shifts, the consequence being that we rarely see each other during the week. I arrive home from day shift; he wakes up for a meal and then heads off for his shift; as he heads home the following morning we exchange headlight flashes and a wave as we pass each other along the highway. But the worst of all is that because he works Friday night, he sleeps away half of Saturday – once again leaving me bored out of my head.

Two weeks later Wayne announces that he's ready to make a go of the business. He's established the local demand; he's designed uniforms, stationery, gained industry membership and commenced advertising. After two weeks of no enquiries, I worry.

The scene changes one afternoon after I arrive home. Wayne uncharacteristically greets me at the door and enthuses, 'I've got a quote tomorrow.'

That doesn't mean much to me. I am happy – without sharing his enthusiasm. A guy can't just start a business and expect it to work straight away. Perhaps I am also touched by jealousy. I wish I could have one ounce of Wayne's vision, tenacity and enthusiasm. He's latched onto an idea and won't let it go until he's moulded and shaped it into a workable concept. He has devoted, once again, more time to his work than to his wife.

I am surprised, and pleased, to learn that his quote has been accepted and that he will start a major garden renovation on the following Monday. He panics and stresses at not having a van to carry stock and tools.

We spend the weekend canvassing car yards and eventually purchase a second-hand van. I fear much of our savings has gone into the venture. I am livid at being refused clothes and household items while he splashes out on tools and materials.

I've never encountered such a situation. My father had happily spent his life in a secure government job – working 50 or more hours per week with fortnightly pay credited straight into his bank account. A life without risk. I do admit though, he was always the same, following life's easy path; no mountains, no valleys, just a flat prairie along which he continues to travel.

Wayne, on the other hand, is not satisfied with his lot. He always wants more. Wants to be the best. I'd not identified that in our initial communications and early days of marriage. I suppose he was treading water. Just as I was.

On Monday, Wayne drives me to work and then heads off to a landscape job. I'm fortunate to arrange a lift home with a colleague, arriving just before Wayne. We have a quick drink and snack before Wayne excuses himself to steal four hours' sleep before heading off to fulfil his night-shift obligation.

I am obviously proud of my husband and the way he's applied himself to his work endeavours. I am less proud of his responsibility to me; I am an employment widow, cast aside in favour of the new love of his life. I have breakfast on my own, lunch on my own and dinner on my own. I long for him to be the real husband I'd dreamt of, the man I'd seen as the proverbial knight in shining armour who'd swept me off my feet from the bare dark world of little to the diamond-encrusted world of plenty.

This continues for months – I don't know how he does it, sleeping for one hour in the morning and three or four at most, in the evening. I hoped it would die a natural death after the first contract, but it just keeps growing. Referrals and phone calls fill his diary until he is booked six weeks' ahead.

I don't see myself lasting six weeks.

It is a demanding situation: he lives for work and I live to spend a few hours with him on the weekend. But even that is compromised because, once again, he starts working on Saturday mornings. 'I'm doing it for us,' he chastises when I challenge him. Now, there is very little 'us' in the marriage. I'm beginning to feel as if I would be better off back in the Philippines. At least there I could grab Mae and bleed my heart out to her, or race home and tell mama all the things a girl in love should never have to tell her mother. Sure, I have my work friends, but they are more acquaintances than friends – certainly not the type I can confide in. And everyone knows what happens with work confidants – they spread secrets faster than an outbreak of Dengue Fever.

I am saved when the two job routine ends abruptly after he is challenged at work about his sign-written van in the company parking lot. Also, his suntan from being outdoors for much of the day – while other night-shifters sleep – attracts undue attention.

He leaves the company after a supervisor claims he might fall asleep on the job and cause an injury to himself or someone else. Pure speculation of course. I know he never would. Wayne is more of a machine than some of the contraptions at work. He is simply robotic; able to do the impossible. Such is his determination. Perhaps he *is* invincible.

His business is now financially stable, so I am ecstatic when he tells me he's finished at the factory and will resort to a conventional life of one job only. I don't know if

Wayne actually understands the notion of 'conventional life', but I am eager to find out. My happiness elevates to levels not yet enjoyed in England. It has taken almost one year.

In fairness though, I must respect his devotion to accrue money sufficient to ensure that we enjoy a better than average lifestyle. He does well. I am proud of him because everything seems to fall into place. I share his happiness and am indirectly rewarded when we move into a new 3 bedroom home, still in Torquay. We spend weekends shopping in distant shopping centres; enjoy Bed and Breakfast escapes around the country; take in new-release movies; tour zoos, markets, festivals, and visit friends we rarely saw because of Wayne sleeping away the weekend. Again I experience the definition of 'happily married'.

I've spent one year adjusting to weather, lifestyle, and the difference between British and Philippine employers and, of course, to the demands of personifying a loving wife. Perhaps that is the hardest part. We know what to expect in the Philippines; our culture is entrenched within us and we understand the nature of our partners. Foreigners though, are different. They grow up with their own culture. Family cohesiveness is rare, or nearly lacking compared to our home life. A Brit (or American or Canadian for that matter) will leave home and see their parents only occasionally. There are very few instances of siblings caring for their parents within their own home – the parents are generally shipped out to retirement villages and care centres. There is a much greater level of independency in western countries than we practice.

It transpires that the more time Wayne spends at home, the more we fight and argue. There is no underlying reason; the slightest thing sets us off. Sometimes our difficulty remains unsolved for days – like I earlier explained about our lengthy spans of silence. Other times it takes only moments to meld into a loving union.

I'm often amazed how time blows away life's confusing issues. It is only months before I'm again racing to the toilet in the mornings.

Wayne's business is flourishing and the future is panning out in the manner I've dreamed of: happiness, children, security, and love. I know it sounds clinical and clichéd, but isn't that what dreams are made of? A snapshot of a lifestyle stolen from the set of a high-budget Hollywood movie? And movies screen peaks and troughs, highs and lows, and excitement and disappointment, just as has my life.

The lows come through Wayne and his work. Perhaps I am selfish and don't express enough gratitude for his devotion, but I find myself spending more and more hours alone. It is now part of my life's cycle. If he isn't out tottering about in someone's house or garden he is doing quotations or sitting at the computer insisting he not be disturbed. Goodness knows what he is doing sometimes, but I know there are tax records to maintain, advertising themes to schedule, business promotion, sundry account-ing, setting in place the foundations of franchising, and probably a whole host of other things I don't know, or, quite frankly, don't even care about – probably because he fails to show enough, or any, interest in me. I know it isn't intentional; that's just the way he is, devoted one hundred percent to every cause – except me, or so I wonder.

Wayne is like most foreigners I've come to know. They are different and more focused on career and accumu-lating wealth and possessions, whereas we just go with the flow. If we can't have something, we accept that – we don't really care. But a foreigner, they're different. They have to have it. They will take out loans to satisfy their materialistic cravings, paying almost the same price again in interest, but at least they'll have what they want. They'll have no savings to speak of, but still go out and buy a new car or wide-screen television because it 'only costs £20.00 per week'. Two years later they've paid double the purchase price – and still have six months to run.

TWELVE

THE BIG SHIFT COMES WHEN I learn he has to go to Canada because of a family problem. It turns out to be much more than a family problem because he is facing criminal offences said to have been committed many years earlier. He hadn't told me about them, although we had touched on his having lived in Canada for much of his life. And there was no real hiding his accent; I actually thought it was American. For those of us who use English as a second language, it is difficult to draw a distinction between the mid-American and Canadian accents.

The first I hear is through a phone call at work. Fortunately (or unfortunately) I am on lunch break. 'Cin, I've just been arrested. I'm on my way to the police station right now. Can you take my passport to the police when you get home? I'll call later to explain.'

I'm emotionally wrecked. "I've been arrested", he says. Right out of the blue. Like a gunshot in the still night. I cry myself into convulsions. I can't shield my tears. Work colleagues surround me. I can't tell them any more than

I've heard from Wayne. I can't focus on work. I take the afternoon off.

I'm barely able to drive home. I walk into the home's emptiness. It is totally different when he is at work and I know he'll be coming home – this time I have no idea of when, or if, he'll be back. I guess I'm going to pay the penalty for having never really thought about much other than the present. *What's he done? How come I never knew?* My mind rewinds to the time I discerned a missing part of Wayne – the chapter locked away in a jewellery box. So there *was* something hidden. No wonder. It must be *really* bad for him to have not told me.

Later in the evening I receive the call. He seems rushed and tells me that he won't be home tonight, or possibly for a few days. He has to appear before a London court where charges will be formalised and a bail application made. He says nothing of the reasons for his arrest other than to say it should be resolved soon; 'I'll tell you when I get home.' My problem is that he can't tell me *when* he'll get home.

I am shocked and desperate. I worry for my security and future, and I worry for Wayne. Having never known anyone in trouble with the police, I suffer a whole new range of emotions, sadness and emptiness. I phone Lena and weep into the phone. I am five months pregnant and bewildered by the surprise revelation. I feel betrayed. I don't know what he's done or what he is supposed to have done.

The following day his Legal Aid lawyer phones and

advises that the bail application had been successful and that Wayne will be released if I pay £1,000 bond. That is close enough to all the money I have, but I agree to pay. I am then felled by the problem of not being able to pay it online. In the days of electronic banking, instant credit, direct debit and a host of other non-personal payment plans, I have to follow the justice system's antiquated manner of accepting payment only in person. I live three hours from London and there is no way I can pay the bail before Friday's 5.00 p.m. deadline. I spend the whole weekend pent up, worrying about Wayne, worrying about the future and worrying about my soon to be born baby.

Admittedly, Wayne isn't doing it easy either, because he is banged up in Wandsworth prison and will remain there until I can get to London and pay the bond money.

I wake on a cold Monday morning, gather my bag and bankbook and head to London. I've never caught a train before because I've always travelled by car with Wayne and work colleagues. I mumble my ticket requirements to a clerk at Torquay railway station and commence what turns out to be a comfortable – and nervous – journey to London. The only inconvenience is the frequent toilet visits, because of my compressed bladder.

I am so far out of my comfort zone when I arrive at Paddington station. I might as well be on Mars – or should that be Venus? Well, it is written that women are from Venus, isn't it? The maps of the Underground rail system look like a spider with its eight legs branching out in every direction. I have no idea what station is the closest to

Westminster Court, or even where the court is relative to where I now stand.

I follow the advice of a helpful ticket-seller and join the post-peak trail to St James's station, waddle to the court, and endure a half-hour wait while paperwork is processed. I can't face the trauma of another train trip, so I hail a taxi to the nearby prison.

Wayne's release makes me happy, but hidden behind that joy is anger and sadness. On the train journey home, I face conflicting emotions: the joy of being reunited and the strain of the unknown future. The carriage window reflects my concern. I hold Wayne's hand. Encourage him to speak. He doesn't.

I imagine the train as a library; its silence and peace-fulness punctured only by the rhythmic click-clack of the carriage wheels rushing over rail joints. Occasionally there is a cacophony of clicking and clanging as the carriage jostles over points and junctions. My thoughts are clanging too, trying to work out how to proceed – how to broach the subject of why Wayne had been arrested. The serene carriage, like the library, allows me to collect thoughts and lose myself in the vivid images presented by my fertile mind. I think the worst. Has he injured or murdered someone? Stolen jewellery or robbed a bank? Why would the police hold him in prison if it were only a minor mater?

Wayne clasps my hand. He gazes through the window, trance-like. His lips quiver. He'll say something in his own time. I feel as if I should at least give him some space after his weekend's ordeal, but I am too panicked and insecure to wait. The future concerns me too. What if he is jailed for a long period? A year? Five years? What will become of me and my unborn child? Alone with only a few friends; no source of income other than welfare because I'd have to give up my job after maternity leave expires. I wouldn't be able to afford the rent on our home or afford to maintain our small car, and once our small savings has been exhausted I'd be at the mercy of welfare. In one sense, that wouldn't be quite so bad because Britain's welfare system is very generous. My immediate problem is that my entitlement is only by the grace of my spouse visa.

I seize the initiative: 'Wayne. We've got to talk. What's happened?'

'I'll tell you later, babes. I'm still shocked.'

'No more shocked than me. They say these things are better if you talk about them.'

'Yeah. I don't know where to start. Some old problems have caught up with me.'

'What is it? What problems?' Tears fall from my cheeks as my view of Wayne as the knight in shining armour morphs to a convict in rusty chains.

'Many years ago I was experimenting with forging Canadian $20.00 banknotes. I spent a few at local shops but became apprehensive and nervous so I never did much with them. On reflection I should have burnt them all, but they were a great job – I must say – and I guess I saved them more for old times' sake than anything else.'

This doesn't sound too bad. Perhaps an envelope of notes has been found. How can ownership be proved? No judge would hand down a conviction over such a historic event. Surely, it would be struck out as a long-forgotten matter. 'Is that all?' I ask.

'All?' Wayne replies. 'There was a box of over $100,000. My ex-wife found it amongst some stuff I'd stashed in the attic before I moved out. She was nervous about it. She didn't phone me to find out what it was or how I came by it; she thought I might have been siphoning off my income so as to not give her as much house-keeping money as she wanted – or felt that she deserved. She also wondered if it could have been left there by a previous owner or occupant. Her sister's got a friend in the police, so she took a few of the banknotes and had him check out the serial numbers to ascertain whether they might have been the proceeds of a robbery.

'The numbers checked out all right, so it didn't take long for a crime member to pronounce that they were, in fact, forgeries. The police rushed through a warrant for my arrest and the short version is, that's what I'm up for: Forging Central Bank of Canada currency. Carries a maximum term of imprisonment of 10 years. Should be winnable because I'm not in what they call 'possession'. That's where the legal argument will start.'

Needless to say, I am flabbergasted. My thoughts race ahead of my processing ability. I wonder if I really know – or knew – Wayne. Obviously not. Sure, we never delved deeply into each other's conscience and past; we were like all new lovers – all sealed in the envelope of beating hearts, newfound emotions and a landscape of the future laying before us with a fine house, children, family pets and the security I'd thought I'd never find back home in the Philippines.

Again, I do not seek to denigrate my family, friends and others back home. I know my family is happy. Most are happy in their own way; it's just that I set myself greater expectations. Perhaps I was delusional. Whether as a result of my own perceived self-importance or pretentiousness, or the influence of American television shows whetting my appetite for large homes and two cars per family, Colgate smiles on everyone from the checkout girl in Walmart to the local trash collectors, I've always set my goal to marry a foreigner. Now, I wonder whether I've done the right thing, or have not been careful enough to choose the right one.

Sure, we are compatible; I can't *truly* complain about our time together – save for the disagreements and arguments that continue to puncture our enjoyment once or twice per week.

We alight the train at Torquay and walk home in silence. The whole exercise has seen the day melt away quicker than an ice cream in the sun. I've wasted hours sitting around watching the administrative wheels of justice turn at the speed of a mill wheel.

At home I throw a barrage of questions about the court case, his weekend in prison and his prediction of what will happen next. I learn that the authorities want him back in Canada to appear in court to answer the charges. Something to do with jurisdiction. That's when I *really* begin to panic.

I panic about what I'll do without Wayne. I'd earlier considered the scenario – but now the prospect seems a distinct possibility. Wayne finally admits that there will be a court case in which the police will apply for what they call 'extradition' – a legal form of removing a person to another country. It has to be approved by the British government; a procedure I later learn will be a mere formality. You'll understand that I become rather cold to Wayne for the next few days, but I gradually accept the predicament and tend to believe him when he convinces me that it will all work out and that there'll be no need for him to return to Canada. The interruption to our life dissolves and we pick up where we left off before his arrest – fortunately with fewer arguments. Pregnancy helps me reconstruct my daily routine, but also promotes eagerness about quickly determining my future.

Peace is shattered days later when our local paper features my husband on its front page: 'Local Businessman Arrested.' The story of my husband's arrest and alleged crime is circulated throughout my new home town. I am too scared to even go shopping. I remain indoors. I'd already taken days off work after the initial shock of Wayne's arrest. On returning to work I saw colleagues flagrantly pass around newspaper cuttings of my fate. I say 'my fate' rather than my husband's because by implication, I am swept up and included in this to nearly the same degree as Wayne. Wayne though, merely soldiers on with work.

_____

The following three months see Wayne attending legal conferences – some in my company. No outcomes predict that Wayne will be able to remain in England. In the midst of all this, the birth of my daughter overshadows all else. At last I have the child I have long craved – but I now lack the security of knowing our future.

Within weeks of the birth, Wayne answers the phone early one morning to hear that he is required at Heathrow Airport on the following Wednesday, at which time he will be escorted by police to Canada. I am devastated, to say the least. The worst-case scenario has happened and we have only one week to put into place our vague contingency plans.

Because we are renting our home, the agent won't renew the lease for fear of not being paid. With difficulty, I secure council assistance in the form of an upstairs shabby room in a boarding house classified as 'emergency accommodation'. My mind is awash with the question of how I will survive without Wayne – not that I am overly dependent on him – but when you've spent more than two years in a relationship, life determines that each person assumes their own tasks and responsibilities, and helps each other both domestically and emotionally. Wayne has always administered the financials and bills. I don't think I've even written a cheque. I am a cash and Automated Teller Machine girl.

The domestic tasks are a breeze; I can handle all that twice over, even considering the extra work I've inherited with the birth of Zoe. What is more difficult, understandably, is severing the emotional ties – I have only a couple of close friends I can count on for help, but I feel they aren't quite close enough to discuss things like breast-feeding, weaning, teething problems and the little peculiarities mothers share about babies and children.

I spend hours – or so it seems – crying out my heart to Mae and mama. I feel like a fool, waiting for the imminent chastisements: We told you so; a foreigner will always hurt you; they're only out for themselves. I try to defend Wayne; he isn't like that and has proven it with his many illustrations of devotion. Sure, I've been hard on his working all hours of the day and night, but when taken in perspective, his energies have all been exerted with the family in mind. He certainly didn't go out splashing money on fancy cars or boats or gambling it away on boys' nights out.

———

On Wednesday morning I drive Wayne to the police station. I kiss him goodbye and then drive to Mal and Lena's home where I spend the remainder of the day sobbing.

THIRTEEN

I HEAR NOTHING FROM WAYNE for nearly five weeks until one morning the phone wakes me at 5.00 a.m. Surprise, relief, excitement, disappointment – a whole range of emotions I am unable to control at the early hour.

'Hi babes. Sorry I haven't been able to contact you. They wouldn't let me make an international call.'

Wayne explains how the Canadian prison authorities refused him access to a phone. In light of what led to his arrest I'm apprehensive. Nevertheless, I listen to his story and learn that he is awaiting a bail application.

That doesn't help me, of course. I am still cooped up in my one-room council accommodation, patiently sitting on a waiting list for a council house or flat. I have to contend with raising Zoe on my own; no one to help change nappies, help with 2.00 a.m. feeds and take over domestic chores of washing and shopping. I have to carry Zoe up and down flights of stairs each time I need to go out, and that is more frequent than I care for because the boredom of living in just one room is excruciating. I have to contend with tenants stealing my food from the communal fridge. Worst of all, I have to contend with the embarrassment and shame of losing my husband, my home and any remaining credibility I had with my friends.

In the city centre of Torquay I am easily identified as Wayne's wife after local papers identified Wayne as having a Filipino wife who'd recently given birth to their first child. How can I not stand out in an English town populated by predominantly 'white' residents? I saw no more than a dozen Filipinos in the whole Torquay district. Of course I could be way off the real mark.

All I can think of is whether to hold hope of reuniting with Wayne, or to 'move on' which is 'today's' terminology for those stuck at the crossroads of life. I don't mean to imply that I'll simply give up on him. I have no idea of how long he'll be away; I do not want to pin my hopes on his impending return, and then suffer when he doesn't. And, strange as it may seem, I have absolutely no desire to race out and snag the next guy who might cast me a sideways glance.

I am also concerned about my future status in Britain because I am nearing the end of the visa's probationary period. I have to remain married to be sure of gaining British citizenship. Once I have that, I know life will be laid out before me because of the British welfare.

I don't want to be totally dependent on welfare though. I see it only as a safety net that affords security and assistance if needed. I insist on maintaining my own pride and that saves me from grovelling at the feet of welfare and pleading for help.

I keep my job, and after the period of maternity leave, return to work part-time. There is a consequent drop in salary, but I love my job, the experience and the camaraderie. Whilst the childcare fees erode most of my wage, there is no way I will sacrifice my job.

The two-year anniversary of my arrival in England draws close. I complete the necessary paperwork to finalise my residency application for full British citizenship. The form requires little detail other than my passport and personal details and the request of a preferred location to attend the ceremony.

The ceremony turns out to be what the British call 'Pomp and Circumstance' – a description of over-the-top pageantry usually reserved for occasions of Royal weddings or other Royal functions like Queen's birthday celebrations or anniversaries. The county's Lord Mayor, resplendent in velvet robes and gold chains with gold medallions dangling across his chest, makes the formal presentation to me and a handful of other immigrants during the short but elaborate service.

That marks another highlight of my life, because while I am a proud Filipino, I am also proud to be granted citizenship in this country where my future is now assured. Zoe, of course, is a British national by birth.

I would like to celebrate my accomplishment with Wayne, but I give little thought to his Canadian dilemma.

Despite receiving occasional letters, my love for him has dissolved. I have the world before me; I have loving friends and work colleagues – and none of them want to see me sad and left alone relying on a pipe dream that Wayne might return.

He keeps me posted as to the progress of his matters, but it seems as if there is always a problem of some sort that results in legal process being delayed, court hearings postponed or rescheduled; solicitors changed. In truth, I wonder if he is stringing me along. It isn't as if there is a strong element of trust between us – whatever there had been was fractured on that fateful day of his arrest.

The final nail in the coffin is hammered home when he writes to advise that he's been convicted and will be in prison for nine years. By then I am insulated by the thick skin I've developed over the preceding twelve months. I've dated a few guys and will venture toward a long-term relationship but strangely have mixed feelings about the finality of divorce.

All this time Zoe is growing up fatherless, a matter easy enough for me to handle, but not, I believe, the ideal way for a baby to acquire a balanced upbringing. I am consoled by the fact that Zoe has no shortage of willing friends to look after her.

My friendship with Mae is stronger than ever. She actually feels guilt for my situation because it was she who landed me my foreigner. I ease her mind by stating that it could have happened to anyone. No matter the nationality; if someone wants to hold secrets close to their chest – for whatever reason – they will do so. However, the problem will be magnified ten times over if or when the secret finally escapes the clutches of its holder.

'Every situation is different,' I tell Mae. 'You've introduced me to a life that I might never have lived, and best of all, I have Zoe.'

With brimming happiness I phone home. Bloody heck – mama is in the same situation. My father has up and left her – no reason and no notice. We share a tear for each other, knowing that we'll each survive in our own way.

FOURTEEN

LIFE OFTEN LEADS US TO isolated crossroads. Stranded beside a multi-signed post, we choose our route. Our choice might be determined by God. Perhaps fate directs us. Or do we simply close our eyes, spin around, and like randomly selecting lotto numbers, commence a journey into blindness?

I wipe my eyes of Wayne's presence in my life.

I remove tokens of our marriage from my home.

I accept the Wayneless future sinking below the horizon.

I see a solicitor and commence divorce proceedings.

And then set my mind to a new foreigner.

ABOUT THE AUTHOR

Jacinta Sequentez writes a variety of novel genres, short stories and poetry. She was born and raised in Cebu, Philippines, and migrated to England in early 2000. She has taken a snapshot of personal and friends' experiences to publish this debut novel.

The Foreigner—Second Chance to be published in May 2017
jacinta.sequentez@gmail.com

www.ingramcontent.com/pod-product-compliance
Lightning Source LLC
Chambersburg PA
CBHW071350170626
46811CB00003B/1065